THE BREVITY OF THE SELVES

LINCOLN PARK

THE BREVITY OF THE SELVES

Copyright © 2007
4465 PReSS

ISBN 978-0-6151-6685-8

WWW.4465PReSS.COM

DEDICATED
TO
STACY LAMB
AND
LILLYAN MCLUSTER

Memories of the past and hopes for the future

Table of
Contents

THE BREVITY OF THE SELVES

PART 1

BIRTH OF THE SELF

1

Candace wiped the tear from her cheek as her train pulled out of Penn Station. She smeared the ink on her one-way ticket somewhat, but she continued to clutch it between her soggy, right forefinger and her late blooming breasts. She didn't know exactly *where* she was going when she left the house, but she had about 67 dollars to play with.

During breakfast, she told her father that she was going to school; even taking her sneakers and gym suit in a separate bag so as to confirm the lie. While she may have been academically advanced, little Candace showed the naiveté of youthful innocence. She actually thought suspicion would be aroused from someone who was used to seeing her leave the house, en route to the same destination, at the same time every morning – with, or without her gym shoes.

She took the subway to Penn Station, because the elevated train that used to run along the avenue (when she was in diapers) had recently been torn down. She thought the removal of the 'el' was nice in a way; because now, the Sun would give some luster to the dull faces of the shoppers, pocket-tugging children, falafel-selling Greeks and white shroud wearing 'Brothers' of the *Ansàaru Allah Community*; who all seemed to spend the vast majority of their lives trying to secure a spot in Hagglers' Heaven.

In some other ways, Candace supposed, she *would* miss her father. Since he was raised in the South, he was still under the merry delusion that the service representatives of the local utility companies would smile at him and chat about the weather when he approached their service counters to pay his bills. But there was no use dwelling on the negative. Candace had an entire *world* to explore – and perhaps, she would find a nice family to live with and feel safe.

Washington D.C. was an eerie, exotic place. That evening, as she strolled aimlessly down any number of unnamed, inconsequential streets, Candace immediately noticed the dense, smooth *whiteness* of all the structures in her range of visual distance. Her eyes were washed with monumental sheets of white alabaster, palest granite, deeply veined marble and limestone bricks. She also noticed that the dense, whiteness of the buildings began to give way to all the *faces* she saw on the street. They were dense, smooth and *black*.

What have I done? What IS this place, she thought. At this point, she was caught in a lockstep with hunger and fatigue on her right flank; with Sunset marching in sync on her left.

Unable to face the homeless shift of the evening wind at her marching feet, Candace approached a simple, black woman and poured her frightened heart onto the woman's coat sleeve.

"I 'speck you c'n stay with us… Mama don't have no problem wif dat. You a pretty little girl. Ever been to DC before? It's *daynj*ous aroun' here – and you got a *real* heavy New York accent."

Accent? Candace wondered about that while she traipsed down the street with her new friend.

"If… if you *want* me to, I can be a housekeeper or something… in exchange for a place to stay," said an enthusiastic Candace to the ignint niggiz standing before her in her new friend's living room. The whole lot of them crowded around her in a fiendish awe; as if they had never seen an actual *person* from New York City – other than in some TV news blurb.

"Well, little girl, I don't think so… " answered the matriarch of the clan. At the same time, she hollered at some of the tiniest kids to tell *them* to stop hollering whilst she was trying to talk to the 'cumpnee'.

" …You *see* I got these kids hollerin' n' screamin' all over the place… these are my *grands*, y'know."

"They're *adorable*, " said Candace, with the appropriately non-nonchalant, middle-classed, background emphasis on the word, *adorable*.

"MA. Maybe she can stay until she can get one of those summer youth jobs, or something," said one of the friendlier adult siblings.

"Word, Ma. She came from New York. Minute she opened her mouth and that *accent* came out, they'd eat her ass *alive* out there on the street."

"Plus she yellow *too*?" added a third adult child.

Mama *hmphed* as she saw Candace cuddling one of the infants.

" Well... the babies seem to take to you, already." The baby in Candace's lap had been passed to her by someone who just happened to be standing around with another baby (*Not to get off topic – but there had to be at least 25 people in that ghetto fabulous house! Niggiz just don't know nothin' about birth control! That's just my personal opinion... back to the story*).

"*God*, Keisha," somebody chimed; " Don't let the baby *drool* all over the girl – somebody take the baby and go change it!"

"Al*right* y'all, that's *enough*," Mama put her foot down and continued; "I'd let her stay, but we don't need *no* more problems from the *po*-leese. Plus, if Social Service finds out, a whole *heap* o' you niggers 'ould get cut the fuck off. Then, y'all'd have to get the hell outa my *house*; but chu *bed* not take none o' my *granbabies* outa here! Let her sit down and have some *kool*aid, right? Then, y'all take her down to the *po*-leese station."

The matriarch waved one of her hands in a swatting motion to clear the living room of all her visible descendants. Then, even though her other hand managed to find it's way to Candace's thigh and pat it as a measure of comfort, the matriarch continued to speak as if Candace weren't in the room, either.

"Y'all hurry up with that *kool*aid. Can't you see this girl problee ain't had nuthin' to eat?"

"You called the police. What is the problem," asked the officer standing in the middle of the ghetto-fly living room. The smell of Law Enforcement did not mix well with the smell of soiled diapers, malt liquor, cigarettes, dirty laundry and cheap, sour hair grease; so the descendants of the matriarch swiftly and quietly recessed into the walls of the rickety, over-bequeathed house.

"This girl need a place to stay, Offisa."

"How old are you, Ma'am?"

"Fourteen," said Candace, with the 'best' side of her face forward. To her, the police officer was *so* fine... she barely managed to escape licking her lips.

"Don't worry, Ma'am. There is a place I can take you for the night; but first I have to check with my supervisor at the station." Thoughtfully, the officer refrained from referring to his superior as *Sergeant*; so as not to frighten the little girl more than she already appeared to be. In the squad car, he became unusually light in his casual conversation with Candace.

"You are smart as *well* as pretty. Too bad you aren't any older. Good girls are hard to find out here, nowadays," he reflected.

Candace followed the officer into the precinct with all the confidence of a person who felt completely protected from harm. There was no *way* that *he* would place her in anyone's home that would hurt her. He was just too nice and good *looking* to do that, she thought. In New York, one of her aunties worked for an agency that had several group homes for adolescents with problems; and Candace was not unaware of the way those city-run homes operated. So, other than the occasional outburst of a belligerent girl in the home, or something, she saw no real conflict with bing placed in a similar sort of environment here in D.C. .

"You realize that we have to classify you as a *fugitive* – but of course, that's only because of the dumb paperwork involved."

Candace began to get suspicious. Especially since her 'escort' had fallen silent and let his Caucasian associate behind the desk do the talking.

"Will I have a *record*?"

"Technically speaking, *yes*. But it's all bullshit. Nothing to worry about. At this point, we'd like you to take a series of sobriety tests, Candace. You don't have to take them if you don't want to – but then we'd have to report on your record that you refused to participate in the tests... "

"... thereby incriminating myself of something else, no doubt. I watch TV, Sir. I get it."

When the tests were done, Candace sat down at an unoccupied desk while the *cute* officer bought her a Pepsi from a nearby soda machine. The white officer sat at his desk, noticeably saddened.

"Of course, *since you watch TV*, you should know that we're going to have to arrest you; but it's just a technicality – a routine procedure, as it were."

"I understand," Candace answered.

She was immediately fingerprinted and cuffed. The cuffs were heavy and cold against her wrists. So cold in fact, that they felt like thick blades trying to lacerate her tender skin. Once the cuffs were locked on, they read Candace her Miranda rights and *she took it like a man.*

When the door closed behind her, Candace stood frozen in the center of the tiny room. She noticed the bed, firstly. It was a green gymnasium mat on a frame; with neither fitted, nor top sheeting to sleep on (*When she saw the mat, Candace laughed, thinking that only this morning she was skipping gym class to ride Amtrak, but could not escape the gym mat to save her life*). There was a lone window, framed with bars and glass that had been blown around chicken wire. Like a lactating breast, a floodlight outside the window spilled the milk of its rays into the hungry mouth of the night. And then – the same mouth spat out the voice of the cop in the squad car: *We're taking you to this place – just for one night.*

She tried to reopen the door of the room, but soon learned that there were no handles or knobs on *her* side; and the hinges to her right meant that she would have to *pull* the door in order to open it. She stared at the door and again, at chicken wire blown into glass. This time the glass was an individual brick; built into the door and positioned at an adult's eye level.

*Candace stood in the center of the dark room with her head tilted upwards towards the Heavens. Jesus didn't do **shit**. He just watched while Knowledge, Wisdom and Understanding punched her right in the mother**fuckin'** face.*

She had been institutionalized... just like that.

From a logical standpoint, she was forced to wonder whether she was in a mental hospital or a correctional facility. But since the real deal at the moment was hardly on the *logical* tip, she fell onto to the gym mat and reached for a gold, filigree cDanny on her neck – that her father had given to her for her last birthday. In a flash, she remembered that upon entry to this strange, looming place, they insisted she remove all her hair combs and jewelry. She began to scratch the unadorned bones of her neckline with nervous speed; releasing a painful wail as she scratched. After a while, she lie in her cold bed of tears and shivered into a helpless slumber.

In the morning, Candace rose with an irritating prick from some dust in her eye.

"Hey, you with the Pro-Keds," yelled someone from the hall, "You gotta wash for breakfast, or you don't *git* none." Candace had no idea her door was ajar while she was sleeping.

"Hey – come back here!"

Nobody responded to Candace's pleas, so she jumped off the gym mat and traipsed into the bathroom; where she got her first look at her neighbors.

"I don't know what it is about the *hair* – but push, pull or drag it in – 'cause the men have to *have* it!"

"What the fuck *you* know 'bout what men have to have," chimed in another girl; "First of all, you ain't *got* no fuckin' hair – and *second* of all, you ain't but fifteen!"

"Yeah, but... " responded the first girl (*as Candace praised her from the side*; "... far as *I* know, *you* the *virgin* in this mothafucka!"

"You bitches are sick," said a third girl as she applied *Sulfur-8,* so carefully to the buckshot-short, nigger-naps of her hair – that if it weren't for the horrible *stench* of that sulfur shit, you would swear before *The Lord Thy God* she was polishing silver.

"Who you?"

Candace was about to sit on one of the toilet seats and realized that everyone's attention was focused on her, so she looked up.

"We *heard* you was from New York. Why you here?"

Candace was amazed. She hadn't said word-one to these heifers, but they all knew where she was from. She just didn't know that to these kids, one look at the black, *Pro-Keds Royals* on her feet, was as if they'd spotted a driver with out-of-state license plates on the street.

"You got a *problem* with New York?" asked Candace, in defense.

"Ain't no need to get no *additood*, bitch. We wear Converses in DC – like Clyde Frazier. Y'all wear Pro-Keds."

"Oh. I heard *that*," Candace said in respectful acknowledgment.

The girls in the lavatory watched Candace curiously as she pulled down her pants to pee; almost as if they thought people in New York pee differently, as well. Finally, one of them spoke up.

"Hey, New York. Don't sit on *that* toilet. *Sunshine* sits on that one... and everybody knows she has VD... "

"Who's *Sunshine*?" Candace asked.

"Me," answered a petite white girl, standing by a sink.

"Y'all talk about this girl in her *face*?" Candace was astonished. Had she landed on the moon last night?

"Naw. It's not like that. She's cool with us and all that – just that the bitch got VD. We don't sit on *nothin'* she sits her ass on."

"I don't have a problem with the things they say about me," said Sunshine, to Candace's complete amazement; "They're my *friends*."

After listening to these lunatics, Candace knew exactly why God placed her in New York City to be raised, instead of Washington, D.C. -- and she made a mental note to thank the shit out of Him, accordingly.

On the surface, Candace appeared not to have paid attention to any of the girls' dire bathroom warnings. She simply spat on the toilet seat in question *(Remember -- this story took place long before the days of the Purell-type, hand sanitizers we use today)* and wiped it off with tissue. Then, she sat down and urinated; albeit with somewhat of a scared conviction.

Some TMI: While she was urinating, she bent her head between her legs to see how yellow her pee was. She remembered her father saying that if a person's pee was too yellow, it meant that they weren't drinking enough water. Candace bent her head even further down into the toilet bowl; feeling in her heart how much she missed her father. The pungent sting of memory mixed up with the urine in the bowl and overpowered her feeble tear duct. Next thing you know, a tear plopped from her chin into the bowl; diluting the thick yellow, just a bit.

In only three days after she arrived at the *Oak Hill* Juvenile Detention Center, Candace had the routine of the cell block down pat:

Up at 7:00am; dressed by 8:30am; roll-call and breakfast until 10:00am; day room until 3:00pm; lockdown until 5:00pm; dinner at 5:30pm; yard play from 7:00pm-8:00pm; day room until10:00pm; night lock at 10:15pm.

Up at 7:00am; dressed by 8:30am; roll-call and breakfast until 10:00am; day room until 3:00pm; lockdown until 5:00pm; dinner at 5:30pm; yard play from 7:00pm-8:00pm; day room until10:00pm; night lock at 10:15pm.

Up at 7:00am; dressed by 8:30am; roll-call and breakfast until 10:00am; day room until 3:00pm; lockdown until 5:00pm; dinner at 5:30pm; yard play from 7:00pm-8:00pm; day room until10:00pm; night lock at 10:15pm. ...

"What *is* it with this kid?" asked the chubby, blue-collar, corn-fed counselor as he stared at Candace and the others in the play yard.

"Who you talkin' 'bout?" asked Miss Eva, the janitress.

"See out there? The girl sitting on the ground. *She* knows the rules. If they're allowed outside, they have to participate in the games like everyone else in th group."

Miss Eva raised a discerning eye at the loud, redneck fellow before her. She knew he meant well with the kids, but it seemed to her that white people in authority, *especially* the ones from the heartland of the country, never *can* seem to shake formalities and page-by-page instructions from their employment manuals – no matter how hard they try. She wondered if he had sex with his wife by-the-book every night, too.

"Sir – maybe she just feels that playin' dodge ball with a buncha people she don't know ain' gon' solve nunna huh problems. From what *I* hear, she's a long way from home, for somebody her age."

"You're in the wrong job, Miss Eva. *You* should be a counselor."

"*Who.* And leave *you* to clean after these kids? *Sho* you wrong!" Miss Eva playfully pushed a can of scouring powder against the counselor's shoulder and went on about her business.

"Don't worry," Sunshine said at breakfast the next day, "I've been through this court before. It ain't nothin' like nobody says."

To say that Candace was nervous about going to court was an impulsive understatement. In fact, she'd easily spent three-and-a-half of the past four weeks, trying her hardest, to isolate and evaluate what wrong she'd done in the eyes of the law by traveling, in a free country, from one state to the next. She ate her *Sugar Pops* with *la bella figura* while the other girls yakked their apprehension and their appetites away.

"Shut up, bitch, you a prostitute," Lakeisha Freeman yelled at Sunshine from acDanny the table.

"I ain'*t* no prostitute! I'm in here for petty larceny!"

"Oh. Okay – you cool, then. What'chu stole?" Lakeisha was comforted.

Part of Candace's mental justification of her surroundings included the sad absorption of the girls and their pea-headed arguments into her daily breakfast ritual; likened unto a warm soppy. As usual, Candace slurped the remaining milk from her tilted cereal bowl while her associates signified to their rights to be called *respected* adolescent criminals.

"I babysat for this woman once, and I stole everything the bitch ain't nailed *down*... "

"Except for the *baby*, I hope," Candace added as she came up from her tilted cereal bowl for air.

"... that was *only* 'cause the baby had colic! She cried too damn much for me," Sunshine said.

Lakeisha finally cut Sunshine some diplomatic slack as the girls finished laughing; "you know, Sunshine – you *white*, I don't *like* you, It's a known fact that you got VD and you can't even *play* like you ain't no *ho* – but'*chu aw-right*. You *aw*-right with me."

Oddly enough, for the first time since she left New York, Candace **felt like she belonged somewhere.** Then, the guards had to come and ruin *everything* by taking her to court.

You know what it was like? While I was writing this, I heard a news story about a picture made by monks and entirely of sand, on the floor of some airport passenger terminal, somewhere. They said that a toddler walked by and destroyed the whole thing in about 30 seconds. From what I recall, the sand picture was so intricate, it had taken the monks about a week to compose. I digress, but there it is. LOL

The ride to the courthouse was long, though nonetheless interesting. Candace was the only girl in the minivan from her particular detention center, *Oak Hill*, but there were quite a few kids from the (*infamous*) *Cedar Knolls* facility. It was easy to distinguish a

juvenile from the *Cedar Knolls* detention center by their hyperactivity –
in concert with sugar-fortified, rebellious attitudes. Altogether, there
were eight juveniles and three (*ripple-reeking, masses of flesh, called*)
guards in the van.

The guard behind the wheel of the van was a Muslim whom
strangers referred to as Ahmed (*pronounced, AK-med*); but the niggers-
in-the-*know* called him Jarvis. *Jarvis Payne*. Jarvis was a character, if
there ever was one; and Candace watched him as if she were his
biological predator. She stalked the movements of Jarvis' eyes as they
shifted from the red traffic signals above; and down to the asses of the
females stepping on the crosswalks in front of the van. As Candace
watched, she noticed how the *age* of the female didn't seem to matter
to Jarvis. When the van hit a bump, her memory leaped to New York
and she hissed aloud.

"Yo! What's your problem?" asked the largest, most doofy looking
guard.

"Stick a fork in some pork, asshole!" Candace yelled back.

"Yo, Jarvis! She's makin' funna your *religion*, man!"

"No she's not," said the man who knew instinctively when he'd
made his way up another girl's skin; "She's telling *you* to shut the fuck
up!" For Jarvis, sex wasn't the fun with these girls. He was well aware
that if the therapists didn't get'em, the counselors would, sooner or
later. Instead, for Jarvis, it was the *intimidation*. The *idea* that he could --
if he wished – was the pus that filled his filthy boil.

When the van arrived at the courthouse, the innocent concentration of fear permeated the soul of even the most guilty child in the group. The kids had to practically be dragged from the vehicle to the massive, white structure that was looming so *Federally* in the middle of the street.

As a successive chain link, the children were led to the lower level of the building. First, they passed by a cell full of funky, obnoxious, irreverent *adult* offenders; then by a most complex and curious communications/ security center. Evidently this center served as the crux of operations for defense of *all* the judicial buildings in the Capitol area. The children froze in awe at the sight, but they were prodded forward by a deluge of towering, Government officials. As they passed the cell which held the grown men, Candace became the target of vile, pedophilic and desperate remarks.

"Look at that *yellow* one. Bitch look like she been through this before."

Candace passed by the vulgar men as they squeezed their genitals and stuck their arms between the cell bars in attempts to grab the children passing by. She walked by with a urinating fright, but refused to flinch. In fact, she tried to gaze directly into the eyes of the evil prisoners, for a moment.

"Bitch – what the *fuck* you lookin' at? You *lookin'*? I'll bend you over and break your *mother*fuckin' *back*, cunt!" the inmate tried to spit on

Candace but the spittle hit a corrections officer, instead. As quickly as possible, the children were whisked into an elevator designed as if it were for transporting non-living freight.

"I'm scared," one of the children confessed.

"You shoulda thoughta that when you were in the street stealin' and showin' your *ass*," said one of the corrections officers. These guards were no fun and the resident pervert, Jarvis, had long returned to *Oak Hill* with the van. Candace peed on herself a little bit as the elevator took them all even *further* down into the Federal earth.

When the elevator stopped, it emptied the fatigued and nervous little passengers into a holding area, much like the back hall of a dog pound. There were cells to the left and to the right. Candace became sick at the sight of the bars... or actually, it may have just been the fluorescent overhead lighting, bouncing off the stark white walls that was getting her dizzy (*After all, none of them had eaten anything since early that morning*). And *got*dam **stainless steel** was *everywhere!* Each cell had a toilet and a sink; plus one slab of elevated steel which was painted industrial green and called a bed. The stainless steel was so smooth and solid that Candace thought about licking it.

Anyways, one of the girls, Patricia, made a beeline to the toilet paper roll and began to make a series of moist, little clumps to throw on the ceiling of the cell she shared with Candace and another girl, Yvette. Not five minutes earlier, the warden instructed instructed the three girls to behave themselves before they went into court. Yvette was caught with a few marijuana seeds, but the warden let it slide.

"I'll let this go, but if I see anything else, you're going to be charged with possession, y'hear?"

"Yes, Ma'am," Yvette answered, humbly.

Candace was fascinated by the way the toilet paper stuck to the ceiling, and tried to construct a clump of her own to throw.

"This is fucked up," she said while she put the finishing touches on a clump; "What if we have to use the bathroom?"

"I ain't usin' no shit shaped for no man, *no* how," responded one of the others; "What they gonna do if we waste all the toilet paper... *charge* us?"

The court hearing went quietly, and Candace was not frightened. Thanks to the appointed advocate's suggestion to the judge that Candace was simply a runaway and not a criminal, the judge allowed her to forego further punishment in juvenile prison. Rather, she was to assimilate into the municipal, group-home environment. She was to be transferred to a home which operated from a townhouse in the Dupont circle area of D.C.. When Candace was returned to the holding cell, she saw Patricia inside, crying.

"They said I have to go back... to *Cedar Knolls*.... " Patricia's tear droplets were as slow and as large as summer clouds at high noon. She looked absolutely *resplendent*; though in a twisted, pitiful sort of way, Candace thought.

"Why?"

Patricia answered with the pure, *teenager-needing-Mommy* contrition she should have shown in the courtroom, "'Cause they charged me with larceny... "

All three of the girls hugged and threw soggy toilet paper clumps up to the ceiling. Just then, Yvette decided to take the marijuana 'roach' she had in her pocket out to smoke it.

"*Huh* uh – oh *shit*, girl. I ain't *catchin'* no more charges today. I'm turnin' you *in*," Patricia said to Yvette with terseness.

Candace didn't speak, but her heart was starting to race. If she was charged as an accessory to smoking dope in a Federal building, she would *never* be able to get anywhere in life!

"Candace – *you* gonna tell on me?"

At that moment, the warden walked back to the holding cell.

"I *smell* something! Which one of you is smoking?"

Nobody spoke.

"If somebody doesn't speak up, you're *all* going to catch a case!"

Candace wanted to rat *so* badly, but even *she* knew that being a snitch was not a good thing to be known for. She decided it worth the risk of being falsely penalized and stayed silent.

"I see," said the warden with impatience; "Well, I saw some seeds earlier in *her* pocket and I let her go – so *she's* the one I'm going to charge."

Yvette was immediately led out of the cell by another corrections officer; and Candace began to pull away from the vice grip of the

District of Columbia's Juvenile Corrections System with a strong arm

of relief.

Two days later, Candace was transferred from the comfort and routine of the juvenile prison to the unknown terrain of a co-ed group home in Dupont Circle (*an upper middle-class section of metropolitan D.C.*); to which she had been assigned by the determination of the court.

"Goodbye, Pro-Keds," and, "Take it easy, New Yawk," were the chants as she retrieved her hair combs and jewelry from the intake supervisor.

"Wha'chu know about New York, anyway," Candace asked as she attempted to open the spit-pasted, manila envelope that had all of her stuff in it. *This shit is ridiculous*, she thought as her frustrated fingers ripped the enormous envelope open and spilled her jewelry into her hands. She had a marquis shaped, natural emerald of one and one half carats weight; set in a raised profile of 18 carat gold, filigree design. She had extremely thin fingers, so this ring would only fit the middle finger of her right hand. She had another ring, too – a ring of faceted sorrow that she wrapped around her left, ring finger. It was a pre-engagement, diamond solitaire round of one third carat; set in a traditional, Tiffany styled, white gold, six-pronged setting.

As Candace slid the diamond ring on her finger, her *Nana Ella's* voice pierced the back of her head with a painful prick:

"You're getting this ring right now, but **this** ring goes to your cousin *Sylvia* when I die." Nana Ella showed off the diamond encrusted band and rubbed her finger across the center of the ring — which was a cushion cut, three carat weight sapphire.

Candace wiped her grandmother's blatant favoritism for Sylvia from her eye — as if a gnat had just flown into it — then she offered the most animated response she could muster to play it off.

"It's a beautiful sapphire, Nana. Fit for a Queen."

"That's why I'll be wearing it until I die. Here. You can have this other one, now."

Candace never got a chance to know her mother; (*save for family folklore; which had it that she was one of the Reverend Dr. Martin Luther King's favorite diversions from the Civil Rights Movement*) or ever escape from Nana Ella's disgusting and dysfunctional descriptions of her least favorite daughter.

"Girl — *after 35 hours of labor with your mother, I couldn't take another minute! Them mothafuckas had to* **induce** *my black ass! Anyway, yo don't look nothin'* **like** *her! Her skin was smoother than a baby's* **butt**; *and she loved walkin' on the back of her* **tennis shoes**! *And she didn't have an* **inch** *of waist! Had more clothes than the law allows! She was a good lookin' thing — if I do say so, myself.*"

Nana Ella died about two years ago; slipping on a piece of ice outside her home in Battle Creek, Michigan. She began her adult life as a chambermaid for a wealthy, ex-Nazi (*it was said*) named Somebody

VonHuber (*who later, changed his name to **Smith***) in Richmond, Virginia. She ended her working days as a retired, oxy-acetylene welder for General Motors. She used to get a kick out of seeing reruns of the movie, *Flashdance*; in that welding 'ballerinas' were just too far fetched – to hear *her* tell it.

*"In **my** day," she would say while she piddled around the house looking for something or other; "14 dollars-an-hour was the **Holy Grail**. We could care less about trying to break the color line at the damn ballet. Hmph."*

The last item of jewelry Candace had in the envelope was a pair of 14 carat gold, hoop-style earrings. In truth, she hated hoop earrings because all the pictures of women in slavery pictures that she had ever seen had the slave girls wearing hoop earrings under their bandannas. At the same time though, she wanted to look at least *somewhat* cool and 'in' with her high school crowd; and absolutely *all* the ghetto girls – Black and Puerto Rican alike – were wearing hoops. However, Candace's hoops actually served to give her *middle* class status – a somewhat reduced, cool -point quotient. That was because the hoops worn by the *other* girls were only hollow, ten carat gold, or heavy gold electroplate (*Nowadays, we call it **vermeil** – but it's the same shit*). Plus, if you were gonna wear hoops back in the day, they' had to be as wide in diameter as *hula* hoops. Candace's hoops could fit inside of a case-quarter. Since she'd never *lived* in the ghetto, it was more-or-less impossible for Candace to get a hold of quite the same merchandise.

The merchants in her neighborhood simply didn't *carry* ghetto shit. Period.

Once Candace put all of her jewelry back on, she went outside of the building and jumped into the waiting van. It was floppy-disk blue, with blue-grey, pleather-edged, cloth seats (*and man – the smell of the pleather would make the head of a dead fish ache!*). Plus, all of the passenger seats were slightly wet because it was snowing outside – and the snow on a person's coat would melt as soon as they got into the van. So, the bottom of the van (*where you put your feet*) was a bit soggy, too.

Oh Lord, Candace thought as she stepped into the van and saw Jarvis' snickering face.

"Hey, Red. Still eatin' pork?"

Candace couldn't ignore the tension, but she didn't know if was sexual, or because the smell of the seats in combination with having to look at the back of Jarvis' *neck* for the whole ride was nauseating her into a quiet submission.

"Hello, *Jarvis*... oh *wow*. Look at the *sunset*." It was about 4:30 in the evening and the Sun was just beginning to go down on the Washington D.C. Area. It was one of those kaleidoscope sky, magical sunsets that are usually only found on 1000-piece jigsaw puzzles and rest-stop, picture postcards. *That's it* – the sunset was turning the correctional facility into an honest-to-goodness, picture postcard! This was the first (*and last*) time that Candace had a chance to see what the

Oak Hill prison looked like in daylight; from the outside and for one last time.

Just for a joule, in the heated beat of her heart, she didn't want to be jolted away from this jacked-up juvvie; this sadistically exquisite place.

Jarvis took the fastest route through to the other side of town; and that took them from end to end of the notorious, *18th Street*; right *smack* into the bleeding heart of the D.C. Ghetto.

"They say that this is the worst part of your nation's capitol, Candace... but this nation is *built* on corruption; and the *revolution* will *not be televised*."

"What's so bad about it, Jarvis... I mean... other than it's kind of run down like Atlantic Avenue in Brooklyn where the elevated train runs."

"Well... I don't know Atlantic Avenue; but look around you. It's time for *unity* in the *community*, my Nubian Queen."

Where was all THAT shit coming from, Candace thought as Jarvis' weird science compelled her to take stock of the people and activities on the street.

"Okay, Jarvis. If you say this is the worst, this is the worst. But all I see are people... *brothas*, actually. What's so bad about that?"

Jarvis remained quiet and let Candace discover that all she was seeing for block after block *were* 'brothas'. On the corners, on the stoops, crossing the green (*and not in between*); riding bikes down the block; walking in and out of the storefronts and pumping the *gasohol* at the gas stations scattered about the strip.

"What's *gasohol*, Jarvis?" Candace was absolutely perplexed.

"Don't tell me that you don't know about the so-called, *energy crisis...* "

" ...of course I do. We had an assignment about it in social studies. President Carter is fighting with the Arabs about barrels of oil."

"And – where do you think *gas* comes from, little lady?" Jarvis was ripe and ready to be plucked for a self-righteously delicious sermon; "It's a petroleum derivative... distillate and such... that's being denied to the *black* man through the systematic dilution and rationing of gas; by mixing it with with an inferior combustible called *alcohol*. But you see, Sister, our people will not be *denied*. We will survive by *any means necessary* – because the *knowledge* of the *wisdom* is the *truth and understanding* of the Original, Asiatic, BLACK MAN."

*My Dear, Dear Reader – you have **got** to know that Candace had the same expression on her face that you have right now – from hearing such a patently, **dumb-assed,** 'Five-Percenter'-type soliloquy. Since Jarvis' heart was in the delivery though, she kept the 'hmphs' to herself.*

"But *Jarvis*. How come I don't see any *women* on the street?"

The gas wasn't the issue, anyway. The issue was that all she saw outside were *brothas*. Tall brothas, short brothas, Hispanic brothas, old brothas, pre-school aged brothas that should be sitting in class somewhere and cute brothers. One brother leaning on an iron banister looked just like Foster Sylvers!

And hot damn! Foster Sylvers was FOYNE!

"All the women are at work, or at the welfare office, or down to *So-Securrty* waiting their turn. If you don't get down there at the crack of dawn, you'll be waiting until the *cows* come home for somebody to deal with your case. And if you a *ho* – you on the job right about now, also," Jarvis said with his mighty and zealous voice of self-appointed authority.

This whole thing had Candace freaked out. Foster Sylvers was a *superstar;* and so was Marlon Jackson (*whom she dumped her crush on Michael Jackson for, once she saw a photo of Marlon, sporting a Kangol. That was* **so** *new York, she thought*) – who both seemed to have lookalikes on every other block she passed. *Weren't these the guys she was supposed to grow up and marry?* Worse yet – are these the only guys who would want to marry *her* someday? *Is this my fuckin'* **destiny**, she asked herself over and over until her tears made two adorable puddles on her chubby cheeks.

Jarvis noticed the whimpering at the back of his neck and decided to lay off the nation-building rhetoric for a moment.

"Why are you crying, dear?"

"*Because* – " Candace exclaimed through a succession of sniffles and whimpers; "I have some posters that I got from *Right On* Magazine of The Jackson 5ive and The Sylvers on my wall at home. When I ever get *back* home, I'm ripping them up!"

"Why do you keep pictures of those pork-eatin' niggers, anyway? You *bet* not let me hear 'bout'chu *swinin'* and *dinin'* over at the halfway place," Jarvis exclaimed.

Candace's eyes were bloodshot and her nose was snotty from all the snuffling she'd been doing; and for once in his life, Jarvis felt stupid.

Realizing what he had done to this little girl, he decided to go out of the way and ride her past the hallowed halls of *Howard University* before taking her to the group home. This way, she could see some 'brothas' in a different environment – and keep her coveted posters of the Jackson 5ive, after all. He was sorry he never got a chance to back her into a broom closet somewhere and fuck her, though. 'Cause now, he wanted to touch her in the worst conceivable way.

As Candace left the dark halls of the juvenile justice system and into the foyer of the conditionally free, it was like a walking blackout. She could have been led over the edge of the Grand Canyon – and she wouldn't have known the difference. She didn't know the people; she didn't know the building; she didn't know the time of day, or the time it takes to say her name (– *which means her senses weren't sharp enough to evoke a narrative from me. I just don't know **what** went on – or what she was feeling until she got to the top of the main staircase of the group home... Sorry..*). Once she left the van and got into the house, Candace was greeted warmly by some of the staff and shown to her assigned bedroom. *Jarvis and his jive instantly faded into the black of her memory.*

"If there's anything you need, one of us will help you. However, since this is your first night here, we'd prefer if you familiarize *yourself* with your immediate surroundings."

"*Civilized* imprisonment," Candace muttered.

"*What* did you say, Miss?"

"Civilized and impressive... my room, that is... um... in relation to where I just came from..."

"Where *did* you just come from?" asked a strange voice in another corner of the room. It was Sunshine.

"You *bitch* – I'll be damned!" Candace hugged Sunshine with all her might and they both plopped down on one of the two, twin-sized beds in the room.

"So how'd *you* escape, Sunshine?"

"See," she began as she picked the jam out from between her toes; "One of the girls got sick in her privates... and they thought I was gonna be the death of everybody. So... and so that's what I was told."

"Well – I don't think you can give anybody VD just because they care if you live or die, so come here." Candace hugged this pitiful white girl again; "*I* care about you, bitch." (*Do you get the idea that Candace was pretty smart for her age? It amazes me every time I tell this story! LOL*).

Candace fell in love with her new room, immediately. It had two sets of French doors for windows which were facing the street. Candace likened them to windows in a mansion, or a castle. Blowing in and out of the doors were long, billowy, ecru colored, panels of chiffon. The panels swerved and swayed like the skirt of a hula dancer (*you know... a sway, then a quick snap to the other direction*) – only in slow motion. Candace was captivated. She sat right up against the bottom of one of the French doors. She let the wind and the curtains hit her in the face as she watched the hazy headlights of Capitol City traffic below. The smell of the cosmopolitan air was absolutely *intoxicating* and Candace never, *ever* wanted to leave that room.

7

"Good afternoon, Candace."

Candace scratched her left forefinger in frustration because for the past two months, she had been searching under every rock in her cavernous mind for the self-esteem all the counselors at the group home seemed to believe she'd lost in the wake of her experience at the juvenile hall. To make matters worse, the counselors were convinced that the non deodorant-wearing, stringy headed, cloudy, bi-focal lens-having psychologist who was standing in her face right now was the one who would help her choose the correct, cranial boulder for her to start digging under.

"I've been here enough times already for you to know how much Ritalin you want to prescribe for me, right?"

"Not quite, I'm afraid," Said Dr. Gale Fowler; the fifth choice of D.C. Corrections to fill their thankless position of *Juvenile Health Executive*. Four other candidates had quickly refused the meager pay, round-robin scheduling and endless courtroom testimonials. Not Fowler. He figured that defending his professional diagnosis in court twice-a-week was well worth it. After all what other job (*with state benefits, to boot*) in the **world** would give a man unfettered access to so many completely disoriented, strikingly beautiful, teenaged girls – all lying on their backs and waiting for help?

Okay – so at this point y'all *know* that rat-bastard put his hands on her. I thought about describing the details here... but y'all don't wanna hear that garbage... *do* you? She's not even **eighteen** in this chapter! Git'yo mind out the gutter!

About three years and an hour after our sad, soiled, little Sistah left Dr. Fowler's aforementioned sicko session, a female guidance counselor at the halfway house summoned Candace to the general office. Since so much time had gone by since Candace was matriculated into the home; the staff felt that it was time they contacted someone in Candace's family. This was to, at the very least, let the family know that Candace was doing well; or at best, get her processed out of there so they could use her bed for another, younger girl who was scheduled to be arriving from *Cedar Knolls*. They knew all *hell* would break loose if the incoming kid didn't have a bed. After all – they were primarily mandated to serve the *local* population of disturbed and distressed teens – not some some New York runaway; who didn't *feel* like being bothered with the rules and regulations handed down to her by the grown-ups in her quasi-privileged life.

"Do you you have any living relatives, Candace?"

Candace just didn't understand why they kept pressing her for information about the adults in her life. In fact, it seemed that the longer she stayed here, the more her life seemed to resemble a giant inquisition:

You wake up, you get grilled; you eat something grilled; you get grilled some more; you go to bed. You wake up, you get grilled; you eat something grilled; you get grilled some more; you go to bed. You wake up, you get grilled; you eat something grilled; you get grilled some more; you get the point.

"I have an Auntie you can call – if that's what this is about." Candace scratched an acne bump on the side of her ear and tried to pop it, but it wasn't ready yet. Neither was she. She just wasn't ready for this new world of blowing draperies and unfamiliar faces to be ruined by the New York known. New York was margarine; sufficient and edible. But this place was *chocolate*; insufficiently delectable. The unknown was good and she wanted some more. But the whole shit was about to get fucked up. *Right the fuck now...* with this stupid phone call to her aunt.

"Come on home, Candace. .. you don't know a *thing* about Washington D.C. ... your father's not mad at you... "

There it is, Candace thought. *He's furious. There's no WAY I'm going home, now!*

"Don't cry, Auntie Aunt. Everybody's nice to me here."

Candace thought to speak longer, but Auntie Aunt commenced to wailing and what-not. She was making a series of shrieking, apoplectic audibles over the phone *that only an Aunt can make*. Fathers don't cry most of the time and mothers would probably be too busy yelling at you to work up much of a dimensional wail. Yes, it was *the Clarion Call of the Aunt* that pierced Candace's telephone ear... and Candace wasn't *having* it! She returned the phone to the female counselor who'd arranged the call in the first place.

"I can't *take* all that crying, Ma'am. Please tell my aunt that I'll talk to her again tomorrow."

"Okay," said the counselor as she rescued Candace's ear from sinking in the auditory quicksand of her crying-ass relative; "What's her name again?"

"Auntie Aunt."

"Hello? Auntie *Ant*? Candace has gone back to her room for the night. She says she'll speak with you tomorrow, *okay*? In the meantime, there are a few things I'd like to ask you, if you don't mind."

"Candy. *Hunny*. This is ridiculous. Come home."

Candace held the phone receiver with a contempt that made her bowels want to move where she stood. Auntie Aunt betrayed her confidence *as only an Aunt can do*; because most kids know not to go to their mothers with secrets. No matter how much they *say* they will understand, moms really don't. When she gets through waxing your ass for being honest, you are *crystal-clear* not to approach your mother with your personal problems *ever again*. This is where the *Aunt* comes in. She knows all your *private* shit... and she stays quiet about it; at least until you hear the voice of the father you ran 200 miles away from, on the other end of the phone receiver you've just been handed.

"Hi, Daddy. I'm okay." The irritated acne bump behind her ear had formed a protective scab, but Candace was at war with it. Every time she pulled off the scab, the pus-filled core of the bump would be attached to the scab. It was painful as all-get-out.

"You know, I got you another poster of Foster Sylvers... um... I didn't... I didn't put it up, so... I thought I'd let you put it up yourself when you get home."

"Come *home*? Daddy – I just heard you making a *date* with my counselor! What are you *doing*?" Candace went *left* at her father's ignoble indecency. All "Pimpin'" seemed to give a fuck about was the mysterious, new pussy (*the counselor*) on the phone. The welfare of his child was an afterthought. Or worse yet, a *catalyst* to this new quest for cunt.

"I only asked her to stop by for a visit -- if she was in the New York area, is all. I had to find *some* way of thanking her for watching over my only *child*... "

" ... Don't go on, Daddy. I'm coming home," responded Candace, dryly. When she hung up the phone, she coughed from the scratchy xerotes of her unseen heart, which pulsed cracked and bleeding; for want of the lotiony lubricant of importance – *or* – perhaps even the slicker, greasier oils of *perceived* import.

9

There was nothing she could do about it. Candace was eighteen now, thus she was to be released from the D.C. Corrections system. The plan was for her to plainly, return to her father's home in New York.

Yeah, right, she thought to herself; *like I'm really going back to the same bullshit that made me jump on an Amtrak without cent-the-first.*

"Is it me, Sunshine, or are adults a sandwich shy of a picnic?"

"I dunno... word. I'm just glad to be getting' out of *here*," Sunshine answered while she continued to pack her duffel bag. They were kicking her out, too. Somehow though, the girls couldn't help feeling fragile. Both were wrought with an ascending sense of apprehension at the prospect of going out into the world on their own.

Today. *Of all days.*

Today – when light from the Sun was completely penetrating and warming the planks of the hardwood floors under their feet; and the dust particles in the air did glorious dances, round and about the glistening sun rays.

Today – when the breeze coming in from the French doors blew the chiffon sheers so fluidly, that the sheers seemed to be trying to say *goodbye, girls.*

Today, *of all days* – when the institutional linens on their twin beds *finally* felt warm and cozy and clean and crisp to the touch.

Today -- when their tenacious tension headaches were totally absent; and the scabs from their incessant, communal acne pickings were healed and hauled away into memory.

Mother*ffff*ucking **Today** -- when the hideous hairdos, deafening monotones and lipstick-smudged files of the guidance counselors' collective essence was as central to Sunshine and Candace's morning mosaic as drinking hot, black coffee in waxy, Wedgwood-blue paper cups (*with the Greek-Key design that says, WE ARE HAPPY TO SERVE YOU*) is to the entire New York City working class.

Today SUCKS, they both thought.

The farewells were appropriately restrained; as neither the girls nor the counselors could act as if they were too concerned about the other. Besides, the new shipment of girls from *Cedar Knolls* had already arrived. Just a few air-kisses to go around, and it was over. *Candace and Sunshine were in the street.*

"Where are we going?"

The group home gave the girls 300 dollars a piece to stay the fuck away.

"Well, I though about Miami – but you know that *Mobil Travel Guide* they had on the coffee table at the halfway house?"

"No... "

"It's... it tells you about all the states and has maps and hotel information and stuff."

"So? What about it?"

(*Candace wouldn't have embraced the thought she held; if she didn't already know that it was practically impossible to offend Sunshine*).

"Like I say – in the pages that talk about Miami, it says to avoid the *Liberty City* section of town."

"Why?" Sunshine asked with interest; "It can't be no more high crime than D.C.."

"That's what *I* thought. So, I dialed one of those 1-800 numbers for hotel reservations and asked them about Liberty City. Turns out, it's not the *crime* they're worried about – It's the *niggers*! That's where the *black* people live! That book ain't nothin' but a guide to show white travelers how to avoid niggers as they travel across the United States!"

Sunshine giggled and said, "Well, *nigger* -- guess we can't go to Miami... 'cause then, I'll have to *avoid* you!"

Both girls belted out hearty, obnoxious laughs, like so:

LOLOLOLOLOLOLOLOLOLOLOLOLOLOL

"Seriously though. I dunno... you comin' with me? After all -- Florida *is* called *The Sunshine* State, you know."

"No, that's okay," Sunshine said with the most phony display of confidence you have *ever* seen. She sat on the bottom step of whatever building they happened to be standing by and put her face in her hands. Candace walked away with a face full of that same, fronting-type attitude; but it was all ruined when she heard a wispy sniffle behind her left ear. She turned right back around and sat down next to Sunshine on the building step.

"I love you, *ho*." Candace lifted Sunshine's face and a bowling ball of a tear rolled down the lanes of her palm; "Now come the fuck *on*. We'll find somewhere to go."

They walked for a bit and reached a subway station called *Dupont Circle*, where they made their descent into the ground on a *monster* escalator! It was the longest escalator ride she had ever been on in her *life*, Candace mused. It seemed to be even longer than the escalator at *Broadway Junction* in Brooklyn! In a moment, the two girls were off into the wild, dark yonder of the subway tunnels. They waited for the train in silence; smitten with the crooning voice of fresh, independence, perhaps; or maybe they were exceptionally quiet because the noise from the passing trains was just too loud to speak over. It was *all* good.

The train stopped at a honeycomb domed station called **THE PENTAGON**. It was somber and assuming. It seemed, Candace thought, that everybody who boarded the train at this stop wore navy trench coats and scowls. Candace accepted that *another-day-another-dollar* living can involve a certain amount of scowling and apathy... no big deal. She stood proudly, on the subway platform with her best friend, Sunshine.

"Sunshine? Sunshine!" Candace tugged on Sunshine's shoulder to see if she was still alive.

Actually, Sunshine was scared to all-get-out and shaking like a leaf. All *she* saw on the subway platform was a boxcar full of big, burly, bruising men with bouffant, burgundy briefcases ready to banish both of the girls to a burning oblivion of hellfire and damnation.

PART 2

DEATH OF THE SELF

Greyhound bus rides are fucking grueling...

That being said, Candace and Sunshine finally made it out of D.C. And found themselves in Fort Lauderdale, Florida. All they had to eat were candy bars and tap water throughout the bus ride; so their pooled money left them just enough to get an apartment share (*Actually, it was a room-to-let in a small apartment just off Sunrise Boulevard and the A1A*) with a loud, self-serving woman who was a piece of fucking *work*! LOL! 24/7, she kept her television on the *TV Shopper's* Club (*All this was before the slick, sales sets of QVC and today's like -- so you can only imagine how makeshift the video feed was. The fastidious freaks who watched shopping channels all day, everyday, back in **that** era are to be forever respected and commended!*).

Suffice it to say, the girls made it a point *never* to be home. Instead, they worked overtime on their respective jobs (*Candace made sure that they had jobs before they reached Florida because she called the famous strip club, SOLID GOLD, from a coin phone along the Greyhound route and told the management that she came from New York and wanted to dance in Florida. The club hired the girls sight unseen*).

"Hey, Tony! You *sure* you wanna put two unknown girls on the roster like that?"

"Look. It's two, new pussies in town from the Big Apple. What's not to hire?"

"If you say so, Boss."

Candace also had a day job, as a back up. She'd been quickly employed at Fort Lauderdale's posh, *Galleria Mall;* by one of the more extravagant, shishi-poopoo, 'anchor' department stores called *Lord & Taylor.* The minute after she was on-boarded, Candace was deeply buried in the musty trunk of the accessories department.

Now, Jehovah *knows* -- that any girl under the age of thirty (in her correct mind) does *not* want to work in *accessories!* Why? *Because.* Every five minutes, you have to recalibrate, re-stack and replenish the table full of *Anne Klein 2* wallets and assortments of bridge (sterling) jewelry on clearance. Never mind the fact that you could vomit voraciously in this vat of vapid, semi-luxury; where clearance is not *clearance* -- it's *reduced.* Every time the overhead fluorescents made Candace blink her eyes, there was some overbearing bitch with a pre-owned (not to be confused with *used*) Mercedes double-parked outside; insisting that she be brought a pair of *whatever*-the-fuck; even though Candace had just spent the previous twenty minutes of her half-hour lunch break explaining ...

"I *assure you,* Ma'am... we dropped the entire line of that hot mess *last* year... "

... or some statement to that effect. Anyway, if there wasn't *one* she-snob sniveling and snickering in front of the accessories counter; there was *another* rank, overweight, wrinkled-linen-clad missy; casually picking up and tossing scarves or belts *(which cost thrice Candace's salary)* towards the fucking floor, for her to continually try to catch before they landed. *Really* -- all Candace could do was stand in front of these rude, crude, cackling cunts and gape. I mean, you *know* – just like Candace knew -- that no new fashion faux-pas, nor excessive accessory would *ever* get these harpy heifers' husbands to stop sleeping with their seventeen-year-old secretaries...

... So, Candace just prayed that one of these old, ugly, uptight bitches would drop a quarter, or something, on the floor in the midst of all their silly, supererogatory spending. That way, she may get a hold of the whole 85 cents she needed to keep from having to walk all the way home from work (*BTW -- Sunshine usually went to the mall after her Solid Gold shift was over; and the girls walked home or took the bus home, together. Sometimes, they walked home hand-in-hand; but that was as far as it went. Sunshine had VD, remember?*).

One November night after her shift at the mall was over, Candace and Sunshine decided that the weather was simply too marvelous for the two of them to waste by fighting for a funky seat on the bus. So, they strolled out of the Galleria and onto the busy street. In a minute or two, they were at the drawbridge which would take them over Florida's *Intra-coastal Waterway* and down to the ocean-splashed sidewalks of the A1A. On this particular night though, the drawbridge was open. Standing at the base of the bridge, was a suffocating mass of teenagers, alcoholics, beach bums, hos, hustlers, retirees; and other people who were simply trying to get home from their own jobs. Before Candace and Sunshine could fully grasp what was going on, they were both hurled into the backside of some nondescript character who relaxed himself on the bridge's pedestrian guardrail. Sunshine was pissed about getting bumped; but she kept quiet.

Candace tried to play it off by taking the fall for the bumping;

"Sorry... we didn't mean to bump you... we don't know what the hell is *happening* here... "

"*Shhh* – you've gotta be *quiet*. They're announcing the next boat," said the dude they bumped into. Then, he inched over on the rail just enough so that the girls could lean on the guard rail (for dear life) and bend their ears toward the waterway.

...And now, the moment you've all been waiting for! SANTA and his pack of Reindeer are floating down the Intra-coastal tonight to remind you that the City of fort Lauderdale treasures the spirit of Christmas! Take time out to do a good deed for... "

"Look! Look! Here they come now," someone in the crowd shouted.

"Who?" asked Sunshine. "The boats?"

Candace looked ahead, and there was a bastion of yachts, row boats, speed boats, sailboats and houseboats and miscellaneous junkets; each covered with gaudy, ghastly displays of sequentially-triggered lighting. There were huge, wooden reindeer, inebriated elves and their clueless spouses; and a boat lit up in the shape of a sled. Inside the 'sled-boat' sat an easily, 300 pound Santa Claus whose flubby face was as black as the bottom of the Great Barrier Reef!

After Santa belted a few, swarthy ho-ho-hos, he leaned his stove-pot belly *clear* over the edge of his boat! *Everybody* on Candace's side of the drawbridge took a split-second to exercise some humanity with a collective gasp. When the split-second was over though, the human concern shit was thrown overboard by *uproarious* laughter; with a round of applause to Santa for, alas, making the water spectacle at least marginally interesting. In fact, it was *especially* funny when the crowd witnessed a few of the tee-totaled elves on the 'sled-boat' swagger, sway and pull Santa's fat, black ass back to safety.

That roly-poly nigger was on his way overboard and into the water; as sure as I'm to blame for this book!

The times when they *did* get to ride home from The Galleria Mall, Candace and Sunshine would ride the Broward County buses as far as they could go on 85 cents and a transfer. If they went south, they could go all the way to the spectacular, *Aventura Mall* in North Miami. If they rode the same bus in a northern direction, they could go past Pompano Beach, Deerfield Beach, Sea Ranch Lakes, Lauderdale-By-The-Sea; and all the way up to Boca Raton (*Boca is the place where people are so stuck on themselves that they would rather walk wherever they have to go than be seen anywhere near a sub-compact vehicle. They have even been known to import fast food workers in on buses from Miami; because it is said that absolutely no one who lives within the city limits of Boca Raton will work for minimum wage*).

As for where they laid their heads at night, well...

... at first, they stayed in a beach-front motel; as far as their small change could carry them. Somehow, they came up with the bright idea that they could save more money by seeking lodging in a shelter. On the A1A bus route, the girls would regularly pass an establishment run by the Catholic Diocese, called *Covenant House* (*Every wayward teen in the United States knows that Covenant House is 'Crash-Pad-Central' for wayward teens*). The physical structure of the *Covenant House* was a white building; reminiscent of a stuccoed, Spanish villa; clay roof tiles, and all. Inside, the administrative offices had bright, orange seating and stank to High Heaven with the ink from thousands upon thousands of itsy-bitsy prayer books.

Candace and Sunshine's intake process began relatively quickly; as there were more a few people waiting to be seen.

"How old are you girls," asked the intake representative; even before they could be seated.

" Uh oh. I didn't realize that this is one of those places where they actually *ask* you your age," Candace whispered to Sunshine; "I'm thinking that if they have to ask, we're gonna haveta lie."

"Nineteen,"the girls answered quickly and simultaneously.

"That's fine – because we only help *teenagers* here. Stay seated and someone will take you girls to your rooms. God protect you.

In a few minutes, Candace and Sunshine were taken to their beds and invited to dinner. The cafeteria was chiefly unmemorable – except for two things. Firstly, there was the cutest, quaintest courtyard directly outside of the cafeteria; accessed by a sliding, glass door. I mean, it was *nothing* like the cavernous, cracked-concrete courtyard crawling with up-and-coming criminals like the one in the D.C. juvenile detention center, *Oak Hill*. Second; the kids in the cafeteria seemed to flock to Candace and Sunshine as if they were Christ, Himself; breaking loaves of bread on the Mount. They thought Candace was *cute*; they wanted *advice*; did Sunshine know how to play *spades*; yap, yap, *yap*; the intake lady is a *bitch*; did either of them want seconds on their *food*; and so on.

"*I* don't know what to say to these people, Candace... honest to fucking God."

"I hate you, Sunshine," said Candace as she sat down, Indian-style, in the courtyard with a bunch of other house residents.

"What were you guys doing before we got here?"

"Nothing," chimed a kid. "We *were* watching the United Negro College telethon; but we got tired of drug-dealing rappers singing about how *School Is The Move*. It's ridiculous."

Another teen added his two cents, "Yeah. Especially if you can't stand rap in the *first* place. You'd never hear *Axl Rose* telling us some garbage about school."

"Ain't that 'cause Axl Rose is usually too high to tell anybody anything at all?"

"Who the fuck is Axl Rose?" asked Sunshine.

"Sweet child o' *mine*... stupid...", Candace answered in the middle of chuckling.

"Ohho*ho! Now* I know who he is," Sunshine recalled, while everybody else rolled around on the courtyard ground in laughter.

Unfortunately, word soon got around the house, that the girls were dancing at *Solid Gold*. In which case, they were kicked out of *Covenant House*. The directors of the house felt that if you were content to work in such a devil's den, you were either on drugs or possessed by a demonic soul, of some kind.

"Since we did not find evidence of illegal substances in your blood; we *must* assume that you are – albeit unconsciously – under the influence of a darker, more evil and ominous magnitude. Of which effect, and inasmuch as the shelter provided you by practicing Catholics is ill-equipped to accommodate such an influence; you two must leave immediately," said Father Bill, the *Covenant House* branch director.

Sunshine and Candace giggled; ignoring the Father's facial suggestion of affront.

"You know, Father," Candace replied; "I had always been under the impression that Christ sought out to heal the *sick*; as the sick would be in most need for healing. Yet, you seem extremely eager to throw two girls with gainful, legal employment, straight out to the street. If you believe we are *possessed*, couldn't you take some of the crucifixes and candles around this place and give us a quick *exorcism*, or something? If you kick us out, won't the devil be raging, unrestrained, in the streets? Or is that, in fact, to be the topic of your sermon at the next mass – PEOPLE WHO SEEK HELP FROM THE DIOCESE AND THE PRIESTS WHO HATE THEM."

"Get out of here, NOW," the Father yelled as he clutched the cross which dangled from his chubby, dandruff-flaked neck.

Don't worry. By this time, our girls had more than enough money to rent another room among the sand, surf and seashells; the teeny-weeny thong bikinis and the many, many, cheap and musty motels of the A1A.

At the *Solid Gold* club, Sunshine was an instant hit.

What'chu thought?

She white!

Besides – she rolled around on the pole and the stage like a damn lizard! Complete white trash form! Anyway, Candace couldn't keep up with all that. The thongs were chafing her butt; the heavy makeup was breaking her face out...

... and other than a 50-dollar bill sandwiched between two singles one time, she just never got the tips like the white girls.

Eventually, Candace left the *Solid Gold* club and went off to dance in one of the management's raunchier clubs, *Thee Doll House (yes – the very club that rockers sang into a classic).* Unlike *Solid Gold,* class was nowhere to be found at *Thee Doll House.* Peacock primping and posing poles on stage were replaced by plastic pools of lukewarm mud; while ladies wallowing in lime *Jell-o* wiggled and jiggled in the middle of the floor. The Broward County executive set and management working class who frequented *Solid Gold* were replaced by Broward County's erstwhile set of most wanted convicts as the regular, happy-hour crowd.

"Are you okay, Hunnie?" asked the club's make-up lady to Candace one random afternoon.

"I'm fine. Why?"

"It's just that you always look so depressed. Are you having boyfriend trouble or something?" The make-up lady was uncouth, but genuine, at least. While she was talking to Candace, she was slurping her way through some kind of concoction she called *soup* -- in the ugliest, little, plaid colored, plastic Thermos. To Candace, the soup looked like pot-luck-to-be-damned; so she politely refused the offering.

"No thank you... it's just that my tips have been pretty lousy, is all."

"I hear ya'. I'm into soups. I can eat soups all day long. Tell you what. I know a guy who is looking for a secretary. Can you type?"

*Candace smiled as she remembered when Auntie Aunt let Candace get down on her **IBM Selectric** for the first time.*

"Yeah... I guess... "

... After the make-up lady's fat, foul and fiendish friend finished fondling, fisting, fucking and farting on Candace in rude and raucous random, he told her that he didn't believe she could really type in the first place. Then, he gave her 100 dollars and some leftover Chinese food from his fridge. When she left the horny toad's slimy stool, she bought a soda from a deli close by and called a cab to get her to

Greyhound. As she sipped the tepid soda in the speeding cab, she closed her eyes and felt a thumbing down in her throat; like the friction of a new pencil eraser against the smooth surface of a grade school desk.

She never saw Sunshine again.

It was *cold as fuck* in Denver when Candace arrived from Florida. *East Coast October* cold. The 'Hawk' was starting to fly about and get agitated; blowing sidewalk debris in your eye and what have you. Here and there, if you listened to the wind, you may get to hear a pedestrian or two, mumbling and scowling about the fallen leaves that would stick to the soles of their shoes.

No one knows exactly what year it was, either. An obscure point back in the mid-1980s would probably be safe conjecture. By this time, everybody Candace knew back in New York City was fresh out of college and tearing up too much shit to know what year they were in from a hole in the ground. Like most 20-somethings on the planet, they all thought they were going to live forever.

Initially, Candace shacked up with her cousin, Marine. Marine stayed at *Chelsea Court;* a pre-war edifice on Pennsylvania Street in the Capitol Hill section of Denver.

"Thanks for letting me crash here, Cuzz."

"No problem. Besides -- Every time you turn around these days, *somebody* is hopping from state to state, finding a new job, renting another apartment; and getting either fired or evicted – etcetera, etcetera. Join the club."

"How do you like Denver?" asked Candace, politely.

"I like it well enough, but I'm actually, only here to see what this nigger Volvo's gonna do."

"Volvo?"

"That's what *I* call him, anyway. His name's actually Abdul."

Volvo was an on-again, off-again boyfriend of Marine's; who had also, for several years, been an on-again, off-again guest of the Denver Department of Corrections. When Marine got to the level of maturity where being an inmate's girl was more of a bane of humiliation than a badge of honor, she theorized that she would cut him off and leave Denver for good. Assuming that Volvo would 'check himself' one day and rejoin the world of tax-paying civilians, Marine would occasionally, make delusional excursions of hope back to Colorado. This time around though, she found Volvo's ass to be squat back in County Jail. It's no *wonder* that she felt that Candace was a most welcome distraction.

By the way -- y'all should remember Marine and her sociopathic man from my last book, **Sculptured Nails and Nappy Hair**. *Haven't read it yet? As far as I know, you can still pick up a copy at www.amazon.com. Whatchu waitin' on?*

" I'm so tired of waiting for him to get his act together!"

"No you aren't, Marine , stop *lyin'*." said a playful Candace, as Marine handed her something to drink.

About a week later, Candace and Marine met Mr. Cleve Hadley. Once again, it was raining like you ain't just *sayin'* it.

They say that Denver has over 300 days of sunshine per year. On the other hand, the weather was so funny out there in the 'Mile High' city that you could have five inches of snow to shovel one day; with not even a jump puddle of slushy in the next.

According to Marine, Cleve Hadley was a friend of Volvo's; who had previously bailed him out of jail.

"Volvo said that Cleve visits him every week at County. *I* don't even visit him *that* much."

"Marine – I'm just not tryin' to *hear* stories about *jail*. Word."

"I heard *that*... I'd forgotten about your stint a few years ago in juvvie. Sorry."

It seemed like the rain was easing up, but Marine was just getting started. " *...Any*way, the reason Cleve is coming by today is to pick up some papers that Volvo left behind. They *say* that he's a Black *millionaire* – and has a home in *Aspen!*"

Since Cleve was an African-American millionaire who was neither an entertainer nor an athlete; he was considered a rarity. Both of the girls were earnestly excited to meet him.

"You know – do you have a resume, Candace? If you do, you should give it to him when he gets here. I mean, you just never *know...*"

"If you have some paper, Marine, I'll have a nice resume in a couple of minutes." The girls laughed and went to see if anything good was on TV.

When Cleve reached Marine's apartment, she introduced him to her cousin, Candace; gave him Volvo's requested paperwork and offered up Candace's ad hoc resume.

"If there's anything we can do for you within the scope of our professional qualifications, we'd be more than happy to help."

Cleve responded to Candace in the affirmative; "You bet. In fact, There's something I need help with right now. Do you have time?"

...as if she didn't have time for a Black, multi-millionaire. Hmph!

TAYLOR COVE - THE PREQUEL

Cleve had some drinks with the girls and mulled over Candace's resume. Once he was comfortable, he proceeded to tell them about his latest project: *Matt Baldwin* and his Rock Band, TAYLOR COVE (*As an aside, you should know that Matt Baldwin was last seen, going by the name of TAYLOR COVE, the individual, on a Ron LaDue infomercial*). Cleve was considering the financing of TAYLOR COVE in a Venture Capital arrangement. He needed a Road Manager for the group to physically oversee the utilization of his finances; should he decide to finance the act in the first place. As it were, Cleve didn't know anything at all about the music industry. Based upon the fact that Candace's resume said that she had previously been involved in music artist management work, Cleve felt that she would be an excellent choice for Road Manager. He also said that if she accepted the position, she would be paid accordingly.

In the meantime, Cleve made note that he enjoyed smoking herb and that he was on his way to the *Montbello* (black) section of Denver to get some. He asked Candace to ride along with him so they could further discuss the business arrangement. They did go along with him to Montbello, but they stayed in the car. They were pretty uneasy because the riff-raff passing by the parked car was checking out the fact that they were alone; in a Cadillac Seville. Plus, she was not thrilled about the idea of sitting in front of a cheeba spot - no matter how nice the exterior looked.

After awhile, Cleve came back to the car. The rain was torrential, now – and Cleve made a complete, soaking *mess* out of the front seat.. They drove back to Marine's house, then talked some more outside in the parked car.

"Candace -- there's a way you can make money with me -- even more quickly than you can through the music management arrangement," Cleve explained.

"How's that?"

"Well, I want to invest in other companies besides TAYLOR COVE."

"Cool. You want to diversify."

"Right on. So if you place an ad in the paper for me, with Marine's phone number and order voicemail service on the phone, I'll cover the charges for setup as well as the monthly maintenance. The ad in the paper would say that we offer business loans to people up to an amount that I would tell you, since I'm the investor."

"Of course," Candace responded, with a touch of boredom.

" You would be the initial contact for the respondents. Your job would be to meet the clients and take applications from them. You would also take $300 from them as an application processing fee. If I approved the loans, you would get a commission on the sale."

"Okay... "

" ... Okay so -- If I reject the loan application, you would still get $125 of the $300 processing fee. Another $50 of the fee would be to regenerate your ad in the paper and pay for your voicemail service; the remaining $125 would go to me."

Cleve said that this was a way that Candace could make quick cash while the Rock tour was being negotiated. Needless to say, she accepted Cleve's offer with great enthusiasm and gratitude.

Later that same week, Marine graciously gave Candace $1,500 in cash to get on her feet. Originally, Candace had plans to return to her father's house in New York City, but she didn't see how she could pass up the opportunity that Cleve offered her. So, she took the $1,500 from Marine and rented a condo apartment in the Capitol Hill section of Denver.

Candace's condo was really nice. It was on *Park Avenue West*; not too far from the downtown area. The exterior of the apartment made Candace feel cozy -- because it was fashioned almost exactly like a Brooklyn brownstone. It was weird though, because the front door to the apartment was in the *back* of the building. In the living room, there was an elevated, non-working fireplace and one wall was covered in brick face.

The kitchen was cute, too. It had a skylight and a counter big enough to slide a couple of bar stools under. Cream-colored, melamine counters

were everywhere (*This isn't a big surprise to you, is it? The entire*

1980's can basically be summed up as **DCCM**; *the Decade of Cream-Colored Melamine.*)! All the doors inside the apartment were classy, mahogany stained, pocket-style, sliding doors. The bedroom had shutter-style, panel doors on a double-closet; and a petite, crystal chandelier was centered gracefully overhead.

The place had wall-to-wall carpeting though, and Candace couldn't afford a vacuum cleaner. So she relied on a manual, carpet-sweeper to clean the floors, instead (*Every time she swept, by the way, she played 'So Far Away' by Dire Straits on her thrift-shop radio until she just couldn't use her finger to rewind the mangled cassette tape, anymore*). That simple, monotonous motion of back-and-forth sweeping across the carpet gave her a feeling of security; as the back-and-forth was a rare and prized constant. She soon sought after this sort of humdrum and ordinary with the fervor of somebody hard left-of-center.

She was at the famous, *Smiley's Laundromat* a couple of weeks later, when she met Art. No, they did not meet while folding clothes at the same table. If you've ever been to *Smiley's*, you already know that trying to fold clothes amongst *that* gaggle of sub-prime borrowers and aggregate reprobates is *resigned impossibility*. Rather, Art tried to mack the rest of Candace's *fabric* softener while she had her back turned; and she called him on it.

"How you *figga*, nigga? How 'bout'chu put my bottle back where you found it. Hmph!"

Art was a disenchanted, college-educated, bifocal wearing crackhead; who had a gift for superfluous gab and the neatest little studio apartment in town. He furnished his place with oddities like tattered, self-standing globes; kitsch like 50's bar glasses from local thrift shops and empty, *Stacy Adams* shoe boxes.

"Ooh, Art. Your place is so *cute.* "

"I shop thrift at reasonable prices."

Art found the way to Candace's camaraderie through the sad bonds of mutual and cooperative cluelessness. One of the things Candace found most endearing about her new friend was that betwixt any sort of random tirade about *the state of the Nation; the World; relationships,* or *diminishing homeownership rates among African-Americans, et. al;* Art would repeat one (*or all*) of the following five phrases like *Clockwork Smurf:*

"... we can *read,* you know... "
"... slavery *is* over... "
"... I don't *work* in the summertime... "
"... I had to seek employment *elsewhere...* "
"... I own stock in *Philadelphia Electric...* "

The particular subject of *relationships* was discussed between Candace and Art more frequently after Art became involved in a relationship of his own. He'd fallen in love -- with a gleeful, ignorant, ghetto hoe named Sonya. He brought her to Candace's house, once.

"*Aaah*. So *you're* the elusive Sonya. I *told* Art that if you didn't come by and socialize, he should dump you." Candace immediately kissed Sonya on the cheek as they entered her apartment.

"I love you, Sonya. Candace is just playin'...."

Everybody went to the living room and parked themselves on the couch; then Candace went to the kitchen to get a few cans of Schlitz Malt (*She knew Art was going to drink it all up, anyway*).

"...Don't lie to me, nigga; where the chips at. Cand*isss* – you got any potato chips?"

Candace sat Indian-style, on the floor, at Art and Sonya's feet. This made it *so* much easier to fall on the floor and roll around in animated laughter whenever Art cracked a joke, or spewed one of his 'famous five' lines. Sitting at the couple's feet in her own home was also Candace's gesture of silent humility and reverence for these, most ordinary friends . *Imagine this child, y'all; on the floor – staring up at these two, damned fools.*

Once everybody was sloshed from all the Schlitz Malt, Art decided that it was time for a philosophical discussion.

"Candace, I've been to college... but you know why I smoke crack?"

"Nigger – don't nobody wanna know why you *toot*," said Sonya, with the sweetest sarcasm.

"I'm sure you're gonna tell me... " Candace replied while spitting out some of her beer in laughter.

"I *toot* – because the minute you decide there has to be a reason for this world is the minute you become too self-important to continue your existence in it... "

"We can *read*, you know," said Candace; while she rolled around on the floor, holding her side in splitting laughter.

Art continued; "Your entire reason for living up until now may have been to to go to the park and sit on a particular bench for five minutes. How the fuck will you EVER know?"

"I don't know. I had to seek employment *elsewhere*. You're *killing* me, Art!" Candace and Sonya were laughing hysterically.

"What if your purpose for living was to shit in your diaper in the middle of the night when you were 3½ weeks old? That would mean that your purpose for living has come to pass and you will spend the remaining years of your life, waiting to die. What the fuck do YOU care?"

"Long as I can have me a little Schlitz Malt while I'm waitin', I don't see a problem with it," Sonya chimed.

"Does *fire* care about all the matching clothes combinations you've worn in your life – or all the dinners you've cooked really well – or all the academic achievements you've accomplished while it's burning your ass alive? No. You get no kudos for doing the right thing. In which case, you have to do exactly what you *feel like* doing."

By this time, Candace was in tears from all the laughing; and she had to pee in the worst way. "Yo! I can't *take* it! You are cracking me the fuck *up*! Fire doesn't give a fuck if you own stock in Philadelphia *Electric*, either! Still doesn't mean you should *schmoke* up your dividends, fool! You're out of control!"

"What does fire have to do with Schlitz?" asked Sonya. The girls paused for a second or two, then burst out laughing again!

When it was time for Art and Sonya to leave, they were *pissy* drunk and full of 'Schlitizified', *joie-de-vivre*. It was the happiest, most extraordinary thing Candace had ever witnessed in her entire life; and she prayed that Art would be her friend forever and ever.

A few days later, Candace started working in earnest, with the Millionaire, Cleve. The first thing she did was place an ad in the classified section of the *Rocky Mountain News*. Since Marine decided to keep the voicemail service on her phone after she moved out, Candace had *her* new phone service in the condo include both, voicemail and dual-ringing services. She placed an ad in the paper with her new, dual-ringing number and resumed working for Cleve. The ad looked like this:

It was at this point that Cleve introduced Candace to the white girl named *Ashley*. Ashley worked for Cleve in the same capacity as Candace; in terms of the loan brokering. Ashley worked through her home in Aurora, CO. Since Ashley and Candace corresponded over the phone daily, they became fast friends.

I mean – from the surface, it was impossible *not* to like Ashley. She looked like *Pippilotta Delicatessa Windowshade Mackrelmint Ephraim's Daughter Longstocking;* off the fabled pages of children's fiction and in the flesh. Fact-and-Fictionistas both had hearty, infectious laughs and smiles that spanned from ear to ear. In Ashley's case though, adulthood replaced flaming red 'Pippi' braids with the cutest, curliest, white-lady 'fro you ever did see (*White ladies called dem 'perms'; but dey was **afros;** don't play*).

For the first couple of weeks after the girls placed their ads in the newspaper, nobody really answered them.

"They say -- that people have to get used to seeing yall's ads in the paper; because it makes'em feel like yuh business is legitmitt," said Cleve, with a slight, southern drawl.

"Oh. Okay."

After that, *Ashley* began to get clients – all day, every day.
What'chu thought?

She white!

Besides – Ashley's tongue rolled around the receiver of her phone and licked appointments out of her ad prospects like a damn lizard!

Where *Candace* made money was through the creation and packaging of business plans. She always had a high mathematical aptitude; and found the calculation of Profit-&-Loss projections to be both, easy and enjoyable. She was especially thrilled if her completed business plans were able to successfully obtain financing for her clients. The agreement was that she keep any and all monies she may receive for preparing the plans because she was doing all the work and not relying on Cleve's lending sources. In actuality though, when Cleve saw Candace making upwards of $900 for each plan she completed, he hurried *up* and decided that he wanted a full 60% of her earnings; leaving Candace with a mere 40%.

"You work for *me* – so – consider it rent for your desk."

"*What* desk, Cleve? We don't even have an office yet!"

"Not *yet*..."

7

TAYLOR COVE

Candace didn't really have time to lament over the fact that she just wasn't getting the loan calls in, the way Ashley was. She kept busy by developing business plans until Cleve arranged for her to *finally* meet Mr. *Matt Baldwin* -- the man whose Rock band she was supposed to manage.

Now, *this* character, Matt, was one for the books! Just a look at his lanky physique and hung-open mouth (*like Demi Moore's in 'GHOST'*) and you *knew* he was never gonna get *no*-pussy-from-no-*where*. You couldn't really listen to anything he had to say either; because you'd be too busy staring in his face, waiting for him to blink. As an irritating measure designed to take control of his conversations, Matt would do this thing – where he'd grunt "(*y*)eah" and whip his head back; as if the person he was talking to was chopped liver (*If you've ever seen a group of young, white guys talking about sports together, you've seen this annoying, head-bobbing ritual in pretty consistent play*).

The truth be told, Matt came from a sad and desperate past. Born on Easter Eve in 1953, Baldwin was thrust into the arms of low-country woe; as he descended from a poor, soggy, Florida Cracker family. After cheap labor in Southeast Florida refried to brown, the Baldwin clan migrated, dispersed and settled at random rest-stops along I-70 and beyond. Matt's branch of the family detoured and went North; first to the Wasatch Mountains of Utah (*where they were run out of town for engineering a scam involving sales of Uranium futures*) and then finally, over to steady auto assembly line work in Detroit.

By this time, Matt was becoming quite the young huckster. Three days after he turned eighteen, he was convicted of Felony theft and was placed on two years' probation. One week the probation was over, he was convicted on concurrent counts of Felony Burglary and Felony Extortion. He served out a five-year sentence in Detroit's Wayne County Jail; then fled to Denver to make a 'fresh" start. He went straight to a Funeral Home and applied for an apprenticeship. The licensing board swiftly and succinctly denied his application because '... *An apprentice funeral director has significant contact with persons in a vulnerable state; and may be called upon to advise distraught and confused persons on matters of finance; or handle significant amount of money for said persons; or come into sensitive or confidential information medical histories. The need for trustworthiness in a funeral director and the director's apprentice cannot be denied."*

Candace met Matt in her apartment. Since the place wasn't quite furnished yet, and Candace had clean, folded clothes all over her couch, they sat on her living room carpet.

"Sorry, Matt; I just moved in... Haven't shopped for furniture, yet."

"No problem. My uncle used to own *Seaman's Furniture* – you know – the nationwide company."

"Great." *Uh-boy*, Candace thought.

My-dog-is-better-than-your-dog aside, Matt was very enthusiastic and prepared for the meeting. He showed Candace a concert performance rider that was as thick as an encyclopedia! To add to the paperwork strewn about Candace's living room floor, he pulled out all part and parcel of supernumerary office supplies (*i.e. - paper clips, push-pins, pencils, pens, pads, magic markers, etc.*), and continued to litter her apartment with his 'presentation'.

- *...Artist is to receive 100% star billing on ALL publicity releases and paid advertisements, including without limitation: programs, flyers, signs, newspaper ads, marquees, tickets, radio spots, TV spots, etc. unless otherwise authorized in writing by ARTIST OR HIS REPRESENTATIVE ..*
- *Purchaser agrees to use only artwork, ad mats, photos and / or promotional materials provided or approved by artist in all advertisements. No product, service, or publication utilizing the name or likeness of Artist ...*

He brought picturesque, brochures of tour buses, complete with written cost-estimates for specific needs. He brought what were then, current rosters of *ICM* and *CAA* signed artists. He brought written cost-estimates for security services as well as a security service contract:

...WHEREAS, Owner desires to purchase security guard protection services for Owner's buildings, grounds, premises, personal property, and personnel, the personnel of the Permanent and Observer missions of the Organization of

*American States ("OAS"), and for guests and other users of Owner's facilities
and services, and,*

> *...WHEREAS Contractor is willing to provide those services, NOW
> THEREFORE, subject to the terms and conditions hereinafter set forth,
> and in consideration of the mutual covenants contained herein, the
> Parties agree as follows...*

Essentially, he presented all types of documentation to indicate the
magnitude of his personal, cash-outlay-to-date. Yet, there were no
documents from any kind of legal or fiduciary establishment.

"OK, so I'm looking at this this stuff. Is your group already signed
with ICM or CAA? What is this for?"

"I just want you to know that we are familiar with the business," Matt
replied; with a tone that seemed to get sharper as Candace inquired.

"No doubt about that – so do you have any legal documents to
support your purchase of any of these buses or anything?"

Matt was irritated; "Ashley has all of that stuff. I went over this with
her."

"Oh *really*? So what do you want from me?"

Matt expressed a desire to 'get the show on the road'.(*In retrospect,
Candace believed that Matt thought his meeting with here to be a waste of time;
because it was clear through his arrogance and over-confidence that he did not
take her seriously, in the least).*

"What I want is – for Cleve to open an account immediately and pay
the balances on the bus, concert hall and security services."

All the documentation Matt had shown Candace up to that point was supposed to be proof that Matt had already paid the 50% deposits required by each aforementioned vendor. That shit was proof of squat.

"This way," he said, "My 'people' can begin to honor some of our 'pre-scheduled' concert dates. "

"You halve pre-scheduled concert dates without a manager or agent in place? How'd you do that?"

"I mean, these are just gigs we had set up contingent on Cleve's go-ahead. I mean, I don't understand... I told all of this to *Ashley.*"

Matt couldn't help himself. He was convinced that Candace would fall for whatever he said; if he showed her enough props. He pulled out stationery with the name of his rock band on it; along with personalized bumper stickers and t-shirts. Then, he slowly and painstakingly dissected the elaborate performance theme and strategy for the 'actual' concert performances. Candace listened. She listened carefully.

...He showed her a drawing roughly executed, of the flag as it was proposed to be made by the committee, and that she saw in it some defects in its proportions and the arrangement and shape of the stars. That she said it was square and a flag should be one third longer than its width, that the stars were scattered promiscuously over the field, and she said they should be either in lines or in some adopted form as a circle, or a star, and that the stars were six-pointed in the drawing, and she said they should be five pointed ...

"By the way Matt, what do you do for a living, normally?" Candace asked.

Matt went on to explain that occupationally, he was a part-time funeral director.

...When GOD in His infinite wisdom has seen fit to call back to His fold a human soul; and when the earthly remains of one beloved must be laid to Eternal sleep; then it becomes the sacred duty of our profession to assist the bereaved living in this; the last task of love for their departed. In carrying out this sacred duty, we will do our part with Sympathy, Dignity and Reverence...

He mentioned that he was also a volunteer fireman. He showed her his fireman's badge.

... I have no ambition in this world but one, and that is to be a fireman. The position may, in the eyes of some, appear to be a lowly one, but we who know the work which a fireman has to do believe that is a noble calling. There is an adage which says that 'Nothing can be destroyed except by fire'. We strive to preserve from destruction the wealth of the world, which is the product of the industry of men, necessary for the comfort of both the rich and the poor. We are the defenders from fire, of the art which has beautified the world, the product of the genius of men and the means of refinement of mankind. But, above all, our proudest endeavour is to save lives of men ~ the work of God Himself. Under the impulse of such thoughts, the nobility of the occupation thrills us and stimulates us to deeds of daring, even at the supreme sacrifice. Such considerations may not strike the average mind, but they are sufficient to fill to the limit our ambition in life and to make us serve the general purpose of human society...

Next, Matt whipped out some fuzzy photos of some clueless dude in a mindlessly conceived, hideously costumed drag and presented it as his central, performance outfit.

There is just no accounting for taste! White boys will wear absolutely anything on stage, Candace thought; "Are you sure you're not trying to be Gene Simmons?"

"Funny, " replied Matt, laconically. He then mentioned that his elaborate, eerie, TAYLOR COVE concert costume was designed to accommodate his fireman's (*military buzz*) haircut.

"You know Candace, I designed the costume , myself."

...an affiliation of amateur,hobbyist, and professional costumers dedicated to the promotion and education of costuming as an art form in all its aspects...

In any case, Cleve told Candace that his lawyers were awaiting her final decision. In which case, Cleve left it up to Candace whether he would finance Matt's group, or not.

"Thanks for showing me your stuff, Matt. You say you gave all your legal papers over to Ashley? Well, I think Cleve wants to finance you; but he's waiting to hear from his lawyers. Okay? You should know something soon."

"Of course. I just... I mean you are a nice girl and everything... but I just don't see why I had to come here."

"You mean because *Ashley* has all your paperwork and everything..."

"Yeah."

Candace *couldn't wait* for this racist to pick up his paper clips and push pins and shit off of her living room floor, and get the fuck out !

Everybody in the office was anxious for Candace to make a decision

regarding TAYLOR COVE; so they waited...

... and they waited

and they waited

and they waited;

as they were certain that

Christmas would soon approach;

etc., etc....

TAYLOR COVE - THE SEQUEL

... until Candace *finally* made her decision in regard to TAYLOR COVE. Such as it happens, she did some research on Matt by utilizing the local library's Usenet.

Usenet is SO cool, she thought.

Candace was shocked to learn that Matt had *three* felony convictions in another state for theft, extortion and burglary. There was no *way* she was going to approve this dude to Cleve; but with a new understanding of the fact that she'd been alone in her apartment with *another* thrice-convicted felon *(Marine's boyfriend, VOLVO, was actually, the first)*, this wasn't the time to do something stupid. Candace wasn't *about* to make this information public. Instead, she felt that she had to find some other way to shut this perpetrating clown down. She went home, and called Cleve at once.

"Cleve, if it's okay with you, I'd like everybody to meet at my apartment, tomorrow night; for, like – a conference-type situation."

"No problem, Candace. Say – is this about that rock group? *Sweet Jesus!* Did you finally make up your mind?" Cleve couldn't stop laughing. It was a nice moment between the two of them, if you *must* know.

"Leemee alone," Candace laughed, too.

"Tell everybody that if they want to eat when they get to my place, they'd better bring some *snacks*, Cleve. Ain't nothin' happenin' in *my* fridge."

"Y'all work for *me* – so I'll cover the snacks."

The following afternoon, Art dragged Candace to his favorite thrift store haunts to get her some 'decent' furniture, in time for her 'meeting'.

"I prefer shopping at thrift stores, Candace. I shop thrift at reasonable prices. I tried to work in a department store once, back in Philadelphia."

"Umm*hmmm*... and I'll *bet* I know what happened. What *hap*pened, Art?"

Here it comes...

"I had to seek employment *elsewhere*."

"*Why*, Art?"

Wait for it...

"They didn't pay enough. I mean, slavery *is* over... "

Candace could hardly contain her joy over having Art in her life.

In fact, she was $s^t_agg_er in_g$ and **shri𝐞king** with laughter; and holding the left side of her gut in the street when she said,

" ...we can *read*, you know!"

"So this is the first time your boss is coming to your crib?"Art asked, after while.

"Yeah; and I wish I had some of dem-*divi*-dends from your shares of *Philadelphia Electric* stocks to furnish it, Fool!" Candace was laughing so hard, she wasn't sure if she get her cheeks to go back down to their regular spot on her face by the time her meeting started! LOL

THE BIG POW-WOW

Cleve, Ashley and Volvo showed up at Candace's place around 7:00 pm and piled into her living room. She couldn't believe that *Volvo* wasn't back in lock-up, though.

"Volvo – how did you get work release at *this* hour? Does Marine know you're in town?"Candace paused; "Never mind. Don't start none – won't *be* none; I don't know *shit*."

Everybody laughed; then the party got started.

"Okay. Cleve, you asked me to manage this guy Matt, and his rock group, TAYLOR COVE, because you are about to invest in his concert tour, right?"

"Yeah... "

"Well, I-mo tell ya' like *this*: I saw concert riders, tour bus price quotes and stadium seating charts. I saw the ICM roster; the CAA roster; the landscape design of *Fiddler's Green*. I saw paper clips, staples, push pins and legal pads; costumes and scissors; sticky notes and legal pads; all the office supplies between here and Kansas City... " Candace took a deep breath and continued; "... but what I *didn't* see was the *album* that Matt's whole concert tour is supposed to be based on."

There was silence, in anticipation and fervent want of continuation.

" I mean, I never heard a single, solitary *cut* from the album! Actually, I can't even tell you if Matt Baldwin can play one note of music! Have you guys heard any of his stuff?"

" Maybe Ashley has," said Cleve.

"Huh-uh. Not me," said Ashley.

"That's *another* thing – that fucker treated me like a wet dishrag while he was here. Apparently, he thinks the *white* girl is his manager and I am her assistant, by default. Ain't *that* a bitch."

Volvo chimed in,"Aw, Candace -- *you* know how white men act in these situations – why are you letting that bother you?"

"No offense against *you*, Ashley; it's just that – why *I* gotta be the flunky and you the smarty -- simply from appearance?"

"I'm sorry, Candace. These guys are stupid," Ashley said with pseudo-empathy. In reality, *Ashley* was the one who led Matt to believe as such. She assumed that Cleve was going to let *her* manage the group, *by the same, racial default.*

"Cleve, do you know if Matt is capable of pulling off a live performance?"

"Huh-uh. Sure don't. He seemed like he was on the up-and-up, though."

Candace continued to ramble; as she was on a roll and everybody's mind was getting blown.

"I mean – you'd figure this guy would have some press clippings from his previous performances, or *something*. Or, maybe an actual receipt from some of these deposits on buses and stuff that he claims to have. Ashley and I could easily confirm any receipts with a couple of phone calls, y'know?"

"Oh yeah. That's a cinch to take care of, Cleve," said Ashley.

People were starting to get restless and it was getting late; so Cleve found a polite way of asking Candace to get to the point and *wrap it up*;

" Damn, girl. You've done some *work* with this thing. So what do you think I should do?"

" Come on, Cleve -- *I* can't tell you what to do with your money -- but I don't see that there's any reference point for you to base a financial investment on."

"What are you saying, Candace?" Cleve was sitting straight up, now.

"What I'm trying to say is – that unless somebody in this room has a chance to witness a studio rehearsal; or hear some music from this guy's group or something, you shouldn't go forward with this... "

The room was quiet, again.

" ... That's just my personal opinion. Like I say -- I'm not looking to side-seat drive, or anything like that." Candace thought a little humble pie might win Cleve over. Sadly, she was beginning to doubt his business acumen, somewhat. She had no formal training in concert management, yet she was able to discern and dissect the deceit at hand. *Couldn't this millionaire do the same?* she thought.

Turns out that Cleve took Candace's recommendation at face value. Before they adjourned the meeting and left her apartment, he called Matt Baldwin on the phone, right there; in front of the group.

"Hey, Matt," Cleve began.

"Hey, Cleve. Are we on for the tour?"

"Check this out. My lawyers won't agree to release funds until I listen to your album, or see you perform in rehearsal."

"Why do you need to listen to my album?"

"They just want me to hear what I'm investing in."

"But you don't even like rock music, you said."

"That's not the point, Matt..." Cleve held the receiver away from his mouth and told the group that Matt was bristling on the other end of the phone.

"Tell him that at the very least, he should bring some tracks to *me* to hear," whispered Candace.

"Hey Matt – can you bring some tracks to *Candace*, then? My lawyers say I can't move until I have proof-of-investment. Candace said you seem to have every thing else under control." Cleve gave Candace a nudge and everyone giggled, softly.

Matt Baldwin went through the roof! "I don't understand. I thought we had this thing arranged. I mean – I *told* you that I would lose the deposits on everything if I can't come up with the balances due. I mean – the tour bus; the stadium... I mean – do you really think I would put my own name and reputation behind a band that couldn't play? That goes without *saying* -- I mean – where is this *coming* from? All of a sudden you need an *album*?"

Cleve was appalled at the disrespect and desperation that Matt was doling out through the phone. He understood then, how the *de facto* subservience thing Matt initially pulled with Candace got under her skin.

"Why do you want me to go through *Candace*? Isn't *Ashley* in charge?"

Evidently, Matt had been talking to Ashley, behind Candace's back this *whole time*. Since Ashley was white, Matt assumed that *she* was the person with the authority in his case and that Candace was simply her assistant. For the life of him, he couldn't understand what a black girl could *possibly* know about rock music, music management, or any sort of sophisticated financing, packaging, or concert tour production. So, it was during this phone call to Matt from Cleve that Matt discovered it was *Candace* who was calling the shots in his case with Cleve. Matt also learned that additional papers he had given to Ashley (*but not to Candace*), to support his argument, had been handed over to Candace by Cleve.

"It's *arranged*... no doubt,"answered Cleve with cool, calm collection; "You said the concert tour was built around promotion of your new album, right? Cool. So check this out, Matt – either you show Candace an album or the deal is off. Simple as that."

When Cleve hung up the phone, everybody said,

"Dayum!"

TAYLOR COVE - THE THREEQUEL

When he got off the phone from speaking to Cleve, Matt immediately recalled how brash and cavalier he had been with Candace when he originally went to her apartment with his materials. So, his behavior towards her began a kind of mangy, mangled metamorphosis.

"Hey, Candi – what's going on?"

Candace could puke behind Matt's phoniness. Like a true professional though, she never let off that this guy nauseated her to no end.

"Hey, Matt – I can't wait to hear some of your tracks!"

He was desperate -- and he constantly begged Candace to influence Cleve's decision in his favor. By the same bent token, he would politely emphasize that there was no need for anyone to see or hear any of his work in order to finance his group. When *that* approach tanked, Matt would blow up Candace's phone and leave a litter of lying-ass messages on her answering machine.

"I'm so sorry, Candace. I can't bring the tapes over to you tonight, because I'm way to play back-up guitar for the John Tesh concert at *Red Rocks*. Check the schedule at the ticket office."

Matt's prevarications became so blatant and so pathetic, that he began saying he was scheduled to play back-up guitar for *whichever* group was appearing at *Red Rocks,* or *Fiddler's Green,* or *Mile High Stadium* or *wherever.* This crap would continue as long as Candace kept insisting on hearing a song from TAYLOR COVE'S alleged album . It was *dumbness,* personified.

One night, after she'd already gone to bed, some bisexual (*by a most **unsolicited** admission*) roommate of Matt's called Candace at her apartment. Right away, the phone conversations got ugly. There was no room for niceties, as the queer quickly got to the point.

"How much is Cleve Hadley paying you." The question was so condescending, it came out of his mouth sounding like a statement; rather than something being asked.

"I don't know who you are, but it's hardly any of your business how much money I make, how I get paid, or what I get paid to do," Candace briskly replied. She had nothing against homosexuals or bisexuals; but there was just no excuse for the *rudeness* and *attitude* – not to mention the *moxie* this guy was dishing to her over the phone.

"It's just that, well – I've done some investigating on Cleve. Are you aware that checks drawn on Cleve's account were no good? I've had his business account checked out."

Candace balked; almost choking from the audacity of this fucker.

"*What*? Have you lost your *got*dam *mind*? Who died and made you Head Accountant?"

"You have *no idea* what you and your associates are involved in. If I were you, I would get out, like, *yesterday*," was the queen's smarty-tarty retort.

During the course of the next hour, or so, the both of them went back and forth. Up and down. Round and round. In and out. On and on. Strangely enough, they wound up not in confrontation at all, but with Candace listening to '*girlfriend's*' personal problems.

"... I'm just saying.... you are such a doll... I had *no idea*... I can't believe you like Bette Midler... you haven't seen *Beaches*? Are you kidding me? Barbara Hershey was to *dye* for... "

Looking back, Candace wished she could have spoken to this man at further length. She believed that this guy knew Matt's intent with Cleve was criminal, but that he was conflicted about the situation. Probably, because he was in love with Matt and was a passive partner in their relationship. Maybe, Matt was *unaware* that this guy was in love with him.

A cool comparison to this conflict would be the romantic dilemma of Will Patton's character in the film, NO WAY OUT. What on Earth is a closeted, government official to do? I love that movie!

It also dawned on Candace that this sweet, talkative pansy was ardently attempting to warn her of what he felt was impending disaster. Could it possibly be in her best interest to be more evaluative of the person she was working for? *Hmmmm......*

Anyway, the *second* the phone call came to a close, Candace shouted, "Hallelujah!" She finally had a *fantastic* way to say fare-the-well to the phony felon with the freaky friend. She called Cleve *instantly*.

"Excuse the late ring, Cleve, but you *have* to know. I *implore* you not to touch TAYLOR COVE with a *ten-foot pole*. Void the contract. Send that motherfucker on his way. **Please**. *You* know I don't call you in the middle of the night like this -- "

"You can call me 24/7, Candace. My wife knows I don't play when it comes to my *work*."

Without further question and with great haste, Cleve terminated his corporate relationship with Matt Baldwin.

12

THE DOWNTOWN OFFICE

Soon after the TAYLOR COVE debacle, Cleve got an office downtown Denver; right on the 16th Street Mall. Everybody was set up in the office. For a salary of $200 per week, Art's woman, Sonya, became the office receptionist. Volvo and Candace shared a single desk, in an open foyer; while the white girl, Ashley, got a private office with a window and a door. She had a personal assistant on salary, as well.

What'chu thought?

She white!

Working in the office was a trip! To the chagrin of Candace's cousin, Marine, Volvo's wife, Kiki, became a regular eyesore in the office (*Kiki is another dysfunctional character you may remember from my last book*). Kiki tried her best to cause friction between the group at the office – pretty much like the ornery contestant on a reality TV show -- but she was ultimately, unsuccessful. Nobody paid her the slightest bit of mind.

Cleve Hadley had a private office in the back of the suite. Everyone had a phone, except Candace. When Cleve hired an affable, older white man named Ernest, to share his back office, Candace was finally given her own phone and line. She also had to share the phone with Volvo, though.

Just like she did in her apartment, Candace made decent money in the office by developing business plans for independent clients. The agreement was the same as before. Candace would keep any and all monies she may receive for preparing the plans; because she was doing all the work and not relying on Cleve's lending sources. In actuality though, just like at her apartment, Cleve hurried *up* and decided that he wanted a full 60% of her earnings; leaving Candace with a mere 40%.

"You work for *me* – so – consider it rent for your desk."

She wasn't in a position to argue with Cleve; because it was, after all, *his* office and *his* phone from where she was working.

"*What* desk, Cleve? You mean the space you have me fighting over with Volvo?"

Besides developing business plans for cash, the way Candace made regular money was through writing stories for the KBKO-AM owned, ROCKY MOUNTAIN PATRIOT PRESS. She knew the editor of the PRESS, Eldon Johnson, through his previous job at the Colorado Black Consortium. She happily accepted his offer to become a staff writer. In addition, She offered the free service of distributing the paper throughout the Downtown Denver business district. Volvo developed a connection for Candace within the Central Denver Library; which allowed Candace to place the PATRIOT PRESS in the library's permanent archives without having to acquire the customary permit.

She might have fucked Eldon, but he had pens in a *pocket*-protector, for goodness sake! If he ate her pussy, he would fog his glasses up! No, it wasn't *happnin' – no time soon* – LOL!

Eventually, she got really let down over at the PATRIOT PRESS. You see, Eldon was so dependent on Candace to fill his pages with articles and content in the paper's initial stages, when the paid ads were at a minimum, that Candace (*due to column-inch mathematics*) wound up getting remunerated much more so than the other writers. Neither the writers, nor KBKO Radio appreciated having to pay her all that money. The patriarch of the radio *station, Dr. Happy-O*, even went so far as to make disparaging comments about how Candace wore 'too much' makeup. These folks could not possibly know the emotional toll they were taking on her heart. She expected this from the TAYLOR COVE guy, perhaps; or some other unconcerned whitey – but her *own* people were crushing her spirit! Wow!

So, after a messy brouhaha, Candace simply stopped writing for the PATRIOT PRESS. It was sad. She wrote like a *dog* for that paper. Those niggers were *cheap* and *hurtful*, is all.

THE GAS MASKS

For a few weeks, business was moving along pretty well in Cleve's office; except for one thing. There were some Kuwaitis downstairs in Suite 318 who were harassing Volvo to get them some gas masks. They were planning to ship them over to Kuwait (--on account of *Operation Desert Shield*; soon to become *Operation Desert Storm)*. They were practically foaming at the mouth and were willing to pay top-dollar for whatever inventory they could get their hands on.

"What you need? You give us good price – eh – we buy. Okay?"

With Cleve's blessing Candace and Volvo started working the phones and shopping around for wholesale masks; but quickly found out that the United States had completely shut down any sales of gas masks until further notice. Volvo dug very deep and found a few manufacturers who were willing to break the law for the right price and security assurances. In particular, Mr. *Qasim Khaled*; an Atlanta trader, was selling upwards of 300 masks each week on the black market.

"I tell you, I have people on *waiting list*. My German masks are gone; my Israeli masks are gone – I got maybe ten left. You want first dibs? No problem."

"You want to sell me the ten you have left?" asked Volvo.

""No," replied Khaled, curtly; "You get for new shipment. I give you low deposit... eh... 40 percent."

Volvo took Mr. Khaled's proposal to Candace. She was sharply struck that her cousin Marine's boyfriend could be such a fucking idiot.

"Damn, Volvo. What do those people downstairs need black-market equipment for -- if the U.S is trying to *help* them?"

"Maybe they are from Iraq instead of Kuwait. But, who *gives* a shit – *I found the masks*! The guy wants a 40 percent deposit, though."

"Volvo – are you out of your fucking *mind*? How you gonna get cash upfront? *You* can't tell these guys that you can't *deliver*... they'll kill us *all*! Those A-rab cats are hard *core*! Besides – what if they were planning a chemical attack? The government could try us for treason!

After thinking about it, Volvo surmised that his 'friends' in the office downstairs in suite 318 were really *Iraqis*; so he simply told them that it was impossible to get around the Government-imposed ban. Even Cleve concurred that if these guys knew of the possibility of getting some masks vis-à-vis our newly formed connections, they might have been killed if they didn't go through with the transactions – whether they had cash up front for the supplier, or not. This type of Import/Export game was *way* over their heads.

Why'd you kill everybody in the house?

'Cause they was home...

THE GOLD DEAL

Then, out of the clear blue-blazing sky, *errr*-body's boat got rocked with **THE GOLD DEAL**. Lord, have *mercy*.

You know, a wise hip-hop rapper once said, "*A fool and his dough will soon split – so when you come across a fool, git all that'chu can git.*" I'm here to *tell* you -- *All-of-the-above* was in effect when **this** madness went down at the Hadley Company!

NOTE:

The diagram on the next page shows the positioning of the players in this deal. Don't laugh - this was my very first time using VISIO - LOL:

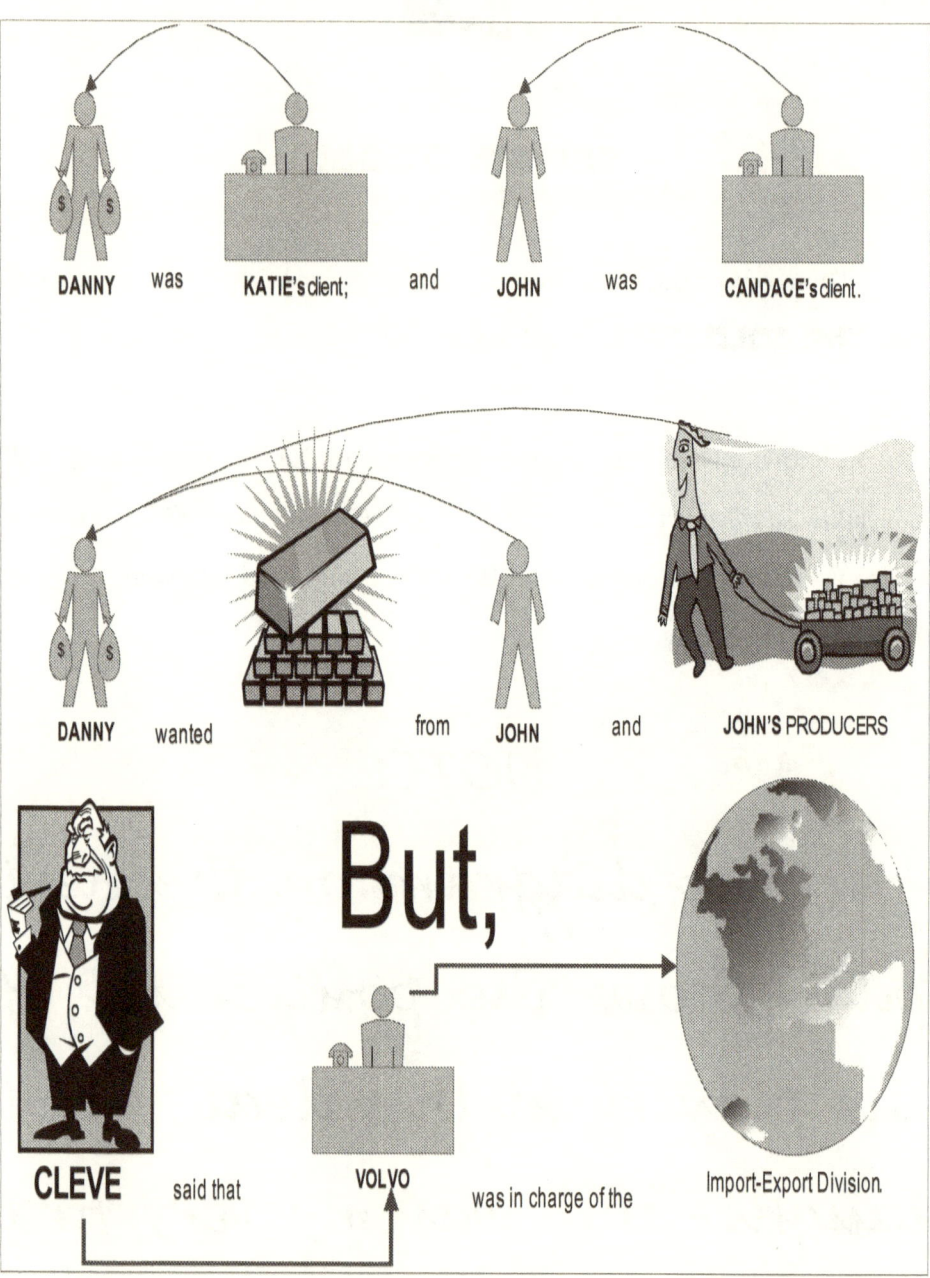

DANNY was KATIE's client; and JOHN was CANDACE's client.

DANNY wanted from JOHN and JOHN'S PRODUCERS

But,

CLEVE said that VOLVO was in charge of the Import-Export Division.

Cleve gave Volvo (*who was placed in a Work-Release program*) the responsibility of overseeing the Import/Export division of the company (*Not that Volvo knew anything about import/export; other than moving 'product' around the Five Points section of Denver; or a brief, but failed business venture Marine told Candace about in one of her incessant, "Volvo, this – Volvo, that" tirades*).

Cleve and Volvo tried to cut Ashley and Candace out of the deal, entirely. *Are you surprised? Like I said – they* **tried** *-- but failure ain't nothin' but a try.*

Ashley told her client, Danny, what Cleve was trying to do to the girls.

"Look, Danny. This guy is trying to cut us out of the deal altogether just because we're girls! Can you *believe* that shit?" *Ashleylotta Delicatessa was hot-to-trot.*

"Is that so?" asked Danny; "I'll take care of this, girls. Don't worry. You two are the ones who put this deal together in the first place – and there is no way this deal is going ahead without you two."

Danny immediately called for a conference with Cleve.

Everybody assembled in the conference room. Volvo rubbed his dick indiscriminately (*the way men do when they think nobody's looking*), and Ashley bit on a soda straw until it cracked. Candace was in another world; her brain bouncing between the bad coffee on her lips; the bad paneling on the walls; why the sea was boiling hot and whether pigs have wings. Suffice it to say, everybody was anxious about what Danny would say. Even cool, calm, collected *Cleve* would finally fidget and fiddle around with his own dick directly before Danny' discussion.

"What's this all about?" Cleve asked.

"Thank you everybody – for coming together on such short notice, said Danny.

"They work for *me*; so no problem," answered Cleve.

"Here's the deal. It has come to my attention that Ashley has been excluded from several of your company's discussions regarding my account. I just want to make it *clear* – that *Ashley* is my representative, here. Absolutely *nothing* can be negotiated by your company, on my behalf, without Ashley."

"Okay," Cleve conceded.

"*Next* – since Ashley is doing the work for me, *Ashley* will get my commission check."

"But... Ashley works for *me*... the House has to get paid, Cleve Hadley kept whining; in order to justify his personal involvement in the gold deal to Danny.

"That's not my problem, Cleve. There's *no way* I'm cutting your House a separate commission check. You and your boy, Volvo, are not significant players in this deal; not for *my* vantage point. So, any cut for your House is entirely up to the discretion of the girls – Ashley and Candace."

Cleve was silent. His ego showed visible bruising; almost as if he had just been admonished with a *'Shut up, bwoyy,'* by a cracker in the Jim Crow South.

Danny continued; "The last thing I want to say is – that Ashley has some new transaction paperwork that I faxed over here to her this morning. Evidently, Candace has already faxed this paperwork over to her client, John. This new paperwork outlines the way Ashley and Candace are to be paid their broker's commissions at close of deal escrow."

Candace took that cue to go potty, but Volvo wasn't going for it. He *remembered* that Candace was faxing something out when he told her earlier that he would kill someone for a million dollars. He'd underestimated her. He wouldn't do it again.

"How much are they supposed to be paid *out*," Volvo asked.

"The residual commissions for each of these girls amounts to approximately ten million dollars apiece; each year, for the next 16 years; depending on the gold trading price at annual payout, of course."

"*Got-dayum*," Cleve exclaimed; "Bbbuttt... you have to *understand* – they work for *me*."

Danny was tired of this exchange and decided to wrap it up, at this point; "We are prepared to negotiate through these two girls, even if they are no longer employees of your company. What I suggest you *do* -- is stop treating them like second-class citizens; by making plans for this deal, behind their backs, that you can't execute. If *I* were in your position, I would be doing everything I could to see that Ashley and Candace *want* to do this deal in your House."

To counteract Cleve's response, Ashley and Candace both threatened to quit their employ at the Hadley Company.

Candace did not participate in the actual negotiation between Buyer and Seller.

After the meeting between Buyer and Seller, Ashley informed Candace that the deal had fallen through. Initially, JOHN said that the gold was being held in Dallas, Texas, in storage. Supposedly, it had already been poured into bars.

In the final meeting, JOHN conceded that the gold was in an Argentine mine and was still in its crude form.

"You're fuckin' *kiddin'* me. What the *fuck* am I supposed to do *now*, Ashley?" Danny shrieked. You could hear him cussing clean cross the hall!

"Dayum. He cussin' that girl like he's *sleepin'* with her, or somethin'," whispered Cleve in Candace's ear.

Supposedly, Danny was badly, perhaps even *mortally* inconvenienced by the physical state of the gold -- because he'd pre-arranged for the gold bars to be sold to his own clientèle. To everyone's amazement, he said that he had taken wires from his clients in advance of seeing the bars (*In the movies, taking advance payments from people usually means someone's going to pop-a-cap, or two, in your ass within the next scene, or two; more or less*).

Nonetheless, Danny - through Ashley -- arranged for negotiations for the crude gold to continue; also including Candace in the private negotiations outside of the Hadley Company.

After the fall of the Hadley Company, it was discovered that Danny was a phony. Not long after he tried to swindle John out of his gold, Danny went to Canada and formed a company called *Tre-R. Tre-R* was soon convicted of deploying -- what is generally considered to be -- one of the most spectacular frauds in the history of mining.

16

THE KATZINGER COMPANY BACK-STORY

Back on the page after you saw my VISIO chart of **THE GOLD DEAL**, I mentioned that Volvo was working with Cleve, in Cleve's Import/Export division. This turned out to be some bullshit mail-order, home-study program from the **Katzinger Company**; which Cleve needed to carry into an office setting to legitimize.

I don't really know how much he spent for his home-study course, but it puts me in mind of the secret decoder kit that the little kid ordered in "A Christmas Story". Lest I digress with this back-story to the point of distress, let me see if I can list the loot that was included in Cleve's kitty from Katzinger:

> ➤ A personalized certificate to hang on the wall; which designates the holder as an 'Import/Export Consultant & Specialist',
> ➤ Three pieces of personalized letterhead and matching envelopes,
> ➤ Five personalized business cards... and...
> ➤ A teeny-tiny piece of **gen-u-ine** Smoky Quartz!

In the 1980's You, too, could have the Katzinger, Home-Study, information packet; all you'd have to do was return an order blank that you were bound to find, on the back of just about every comic book in America!

By the early 1990's though, the Katzinger Company was slapped with a $50,000.00 civil penalty for violation of a FTC cease-and-desist order. Said order addressed charges of deceptive, misleading and false advertising and guarantee of home-business success; via-their systems. According to court documents detailing the violation charges, Katzinger's print and television advertising campaigns promoted the company's work-from-home course with sensational claims such as:

> "How would you like to earn substantial income right from the comfort of your own home? ... Living a luxurious lifestyle with long-term security for you and your family."

> "On my first customer during my first day with Katzinger Home Study Course, I made 12 thousand dollars in profit."

> "I started off with $250 that my husband gave me. Last year, thanks to Katzinger, I earned over $350,000.00

> My nephew, Keith, may not be a brain surgeon, but with the help of the Katzinger Home Study Course, he has launched a smart business that brings him in a brain surgeon's salary!"

The aforementioned FTC order remains in effect until 2017; last anybody heard.

17

Candace went into *The Hadley Company* with good and honest intentions. She was particularly inspired because she *thought* she was working for one of the few, bona-fide, African-American, non-entertainment-based, entrepreneurial ka*blillion*aires in the *U-S*-of-this-here-*A* (*besides Oprah, of course; Reginald Lewis and Bob Johnson*)! If anything, Candace wanted to work *harder* so that he would help her to become that same type of successful professional.

Back at The Hadley Company, Candace's telephone respondents were not giving her the required processing fee; so she never made any money in that specific fashion. Cleve Hadley assured Candace, on more than one occasion, that he would cover her apartment rent for her if her business did not pick up.

All that talk about helping with her rent ended up being bullshit, you know -- and Candace was pissed! She was fit to be tied! **THE GOLD DEAL** was a bust, and Cleve was using the money she *did* manage to make (*from developing business plans*) to *meet his payroll!* The list of moochers would include:

- *Sonya and Ernest*
- *Ashley's personal assistant*
- *Volvo (of all things!)*

To make matters worse, she read an article in the newspaper that said:

- *charging a processing fee for loans or loan applications is illegal in the State of Colorado.*

Worried, Candace decided to approach Cleve with the article and find out if the office was in any kind of trouble.

"We're exempt from the ruling because this company was chartered through a Massachusetts incorporation," he said.

"Al*right*ie, then... "

Candace closed her eyes that night, and was transported to a beach with Bette Midler, Barbara Hershey and that little fag friend of Matt Baldwin's. She was covered in sand and shaking from head to toe.

18

"We're exempt from the ruling because this company was chartered through a Massachusetts incorporation," Cleve said.

Here's the problem with that:

Marv Searle, Denver's dynamic, debonair and *disgustingly* conceited District Attorney, didn't give a damn *where* Cleve Hadley was incorporated. It could have been in Denver, Delaware, Detroit or the Delta Quadrant of *Deep Space 12*, for all Marv Searle knew, or cared. This 'processing-fee' shit had the *audacity* to be going down on *his* turf; and any frivolity that got in the way of his ambition to become Mayor of Denver, Colorado was going to get squashed like a roach on a housing project stairwell!

"Mr. Hadley? This is Dan Roquefort; Assistant District Attorney. We're calling to investigate complaints we've logged from some of your unsatisfied customers."

"What?" The complaints were against Cleve and Ashley; and Cleve knew it... he was busted...

"It is our understanding that none of your clients seem to be getting any loans approved and everyone has paid you a $300 application processing fee for those loans."

The D.A. called Cleve's entire staff in, one at a time, for rounds and rounds of ridiculous *ringoleevio* that his office preferred to refer to as *questioning*.

"What the fuck else do these people *want*?"

"Dunno, Cleve. Whatja do?"

Following suit with their unique, *D-A-dar*, were the local TV stations. One by one, the stations' field anchors harassed and harangued the whole Hadley staff for inside information (*If she saw TV vans or crews outside of the office building, Candace knew jump on the free, 16th Street shuttle bus – down to Larimer Street; or back the opposite way, over to Colfax Avenue*).

When it was Candace's turn to visit the District Attorney's office, she had no prior knowledge of any of the allegations against Ashley or Cleve. On the other hand, Ashley was jamming! She got client after client, check after check! *It was alleged that she was forging Cleve's signature to the checks and cashing them on her own.*

Since none of the respondents to *Candace's* newspaper ad ever gave her any money though, the D.A. no longer held Candace suspect in any criminal activity. But she *was* told, in no uncertain terms, that if she was still working for the Hadley Company when they brought it down, she would be arrested right along with everybody else.

The D.A. said, "I know that you didn't have anything to do with this, Candace, but you'd better get out now, because we're going in. **We're**

taking him down. And just so you know – if you're in there when we take him down, *you're going down, too.*"

Candace was scared to shit. She knew that any future encounter with anybody's *Department of Corrections* would not involve, dodge ball, billowy chiffon curtains, Jarvis' Islamic soliloquies or chicken-wired windows. She high-tailed her ass back to the office and *immediately* began clearing her desk.

"Where *you* goin' ?"

"The flip away from *here*," Candace replied while she stuffed her office supplies and what-not into a small, cardboard box.

That night, she couldn't sleep. Every time she shut her eyes, she got hit with a dark red, hard rubber, dodge ball from the **Oak Hill** *courtyard.*

"I have an idea," somebody said.

"What."

"Since our days are numbered here at *The Hadley Company*, I know a way we can each pocket at least *50* bucks out of this guy... "

"How?"

"Cleve rented beepers for everybody, right? We can report them lost, then mail them back in to the beeper company. This way, we can collect the reward money they offer... um... when you find a lost beeper."

FYI -- that shit actually worked!

As for the rest of the people who worked at *The Hadley Company*, there were rough times to be had. Ashley and Candace were both being evicted from their respective apartments; Volvo's work-release was terminated and he returned to convict population in prison; Ashley's assistant returned to her parents' home in Phoenix, AZ; Dan was in a car accident, fell behind on his mortgage payments AND suffered a stroke!

But wait... there's more! Cleve Hadley never paid any of his *suppliers;* neither for furniture, nor fixtures, nor paper, nor pens nor photocopies! What made the whole scene so specially sour was that Cleve's office was the only office run by African-Americans in the entire building! Mr. Cleve Hadley and his sweet, slinky business operating style was a completely corrupt, rusted, encrusted embarrassment!

"Set the black race back 200 years," some would say, later on.

They couldn't stop the evictions, but Cleve Hadley's staff bought some time through a letter Candace composed and of which they all forced Cleve to sign. The letter (*Due to quick thinking and composition on Candace's part*), stated basically, this:

To Whom It May Concern:
Due to company restructuring, payroll has been suspended. Please contact Mr. Cleve Hadley if you have further questions.

This letter enabled Candace to buy two more weeks in her apartment. Nevertheless, she was inevitably evicted; just two days before Christmas. Christmas Eve *Eve*, if you will.

19

The eviction was cold. Christmasy, carolly cold. Cold blooded. Cold, damn blooded as a parent charging their child rent to sleep in the bed that child was raised in; the day after that child turns 18

Looks like that Capitol-City convict got a chance to break Candace's back, at long last.

"Art, I have absolutely *nowhere* to go. Can I sleep on your floor?"

"I'm getting evicted, too – so we can all stay at Sonya's."

"Oh for God's sake. Your crackhead girlfriend? *They don't pay enough.*"

Hey, Jesus! Why you keep ignoring me, bitch, Candace thought. She battled the tears streaming into her mouth with the heartiest laugh you've

ever, in your life read about.

Seriously. I mean, this girl laughed like her heart was being stabbed through with the blade of a rusty shovel!

The next afternoon, the shit 'hit the fan', so to speak. *The Hadley Company* was engulfed in the furious, white flames of three, Assistant District Attorneys. The whole office, and its contents thereof, were sealed off with red, crime-scene tape and the *Black Savior*, the *Millionaire*

Extrordinaire, Cleve Hadley, was led out in heavy, humiliating, humongozoid handcuffs. Unfortunately, Cleve was under the impression that *Candace* was the one who brought him down – because she left the office so abruptly the day before. Truth was, the District Attorney simply played everyone against the other; to see who would roll (*This strategy sound familiar? You can see this tactic played out on any one of those 'TV-Lawyer' shows every week God sends*).

Before everything went down, I can't lie. Candace never *ever* snitched on Cleve; but once she was told to leave, she *did* begin to sabotage some of the newer client accounts she had at Cleve's company and encouraged those clients to defect with her. Ashley and Volvo were supposed to follow in-kind; then form a partnership with Candace in a new venture. To her dismay, they seemed to want *her* to do all of the start-up legwork by herself. She did, and thusly formed a new loan brokerage, SOUTHSIDE FINANCIAL SYSTEMS, without either of them.

*FYI -- As it turns out, it was the perky-jerky white girl, **Ashley**, who initiated the plot to have Cleve busted. Cleve never suspected **her** for a minute!*

What'chu thought?
She white!

PART 3

THE BREVITY OF THE SELVES

Greyhound bus rides are fucking grueling...

... That being said, Candace made sure to sit in the front seat of the bus, next to the passenger door. She chose that seat not so much as for a respect to Rosa Parks; as to be able to hear the stories she knew the driver would be compelled to tell anybody he thought was listening. *Don't **act** like you don't **know** – it's an established **fact** that bus drivers can ring your ears like they were the Liberty Bell with some of the sudsy tales that foam out of their mouths on those long, bus trips!*

"Okay – and so you're saying that they gave you this route after Trailways merged with Greyhound."

"No," said the driver as the bus zoomed by the Delaware Water Gap; "It wasn't a *merge*. Greyhound just took over. So, let's say – you had a driver who put in 16 years at Trailways. They would lose *all their seniority* when Greyhound took over. **And** – I'll *tell* ya'. Losing the pension and retirement benefits isn't what sticks in *my* craw. It's them *Greyhound* boys keeping all the good *routes*! If I knew I was gonna spend the rest of my life running up and down I-95, I might've tried going to college!"

Candace was speechless. They were nowhere near I-95.

"I only drive bus on the side, anymore. The *money* is in *credit*, nowadays. You give me 65 dollars, I'll erase *all* your credit problems."

"Gee, Buddy,"somebody yelled from further back in the bus; "If I had 65 dollars, I wouldn't *need* credit. I'd have *cash*." Most everybody laughed except for Candace. See, there was a Quaker gentleman seated next to her since Johnstown; who was dressed in a heavy, stinky, linty black felt coat. He smelled *really bad*. Not bad*ly* -- pure, dee-vine **bad**. Candace vowed to herself that she would never, *ever* have an occasion in her life that would call for her to use homemade soap. *Clearly*, it didn't work for all those who professed to use it.

By late afternoon, Candace had traveled out of a decade, out of D.C., out of Denver and found herself full circle, in New York City. Square got the circle though; because she was square out of money, out of sorts and out of touch.

*Shit. I'm **so** sore from sittin' on that bus...*

While she waited outside the bus terminal for a cab, her mind jumped into each of the other passing cars.

Why did I bother to eat my spinach at home? Why the fuck did I ever finish my homework in school? Does New York City care? Fuuckk! I stepped in gummm!

All she had to eat were candy bars and tap water throughout the whole, two and one-half day bus ride. So when she finally caught a cab, Candace asked the cab driver to take her to a nice coffee shop.

"I don't care where. Just like; can you take me somewhere where they have a decent restroom?"

The cabbie said he knew a place where they made a mean, Yankee Pot Roast; so Candace ended up at the *Washington Square* Restaurant in the West Village.

"Sit anywhere you want, Doll," said somebody from behind the counter as Candace walked in.

She slid into a booth in the NO SMOKING section, next to a bunch of elderly, Jewish ladies. The vinyl seating of the booth felt uncomfortably damp to Candace's back, but what-the-hell. Whadd'yagonnado? Meanwhile, the Jewish ladies in the adjoining booth seemed to be placing high, soup-slurping, danish-waving stakes on whose ophthalmologist was better than whose.

"My doctor lives in Cedarhurst, but he practices at St. Vincent's."

"I know St. Vincent's – they're no good, I tell ya'! Mye doctor works at New York Hospital on Tuesdays and Fridays. Then, every third Wednesday he goes to LaGuardia in Forest Hills. He refuses to work in Catholic hospitals!"

"Catholic, shmatholic; what difference does it make? My mother almost died at Columbia Presbyterian! Thank God we took her out of there!"

"So, what happened to her?"

*"Murray was the first one to find out. She died at home. Whadd'ya **mean**, what happened."*

Candace sighed. As a young woman, smack dab in the middle of the largest city on the planet, she couldn't shake the feeling like she was just a frightened runaway in a dark room; saying a prayer to Jesus that was just as old and worn as the coffee shop menu in her hand. She knew she finally, had to leave the vicarious company of these good people and go home.

Just then, Candace looked out of the coffee shop window, over towards Washington Square Park. Her eyes transfixed on a couple of *Brothas*. Brothas on a park bench. Brothas on a park bench in the cold. Catching herself staring, she looked away from the window; only to see old Jarvis from D.C., jacking off and talking smack in the bottom of her coffee cup. Since *that* vulgar visual quickly killed her appetite for Yankee Pot Roast, Candace decided to leave the restaurant and go window-shopping on West 8th street for awhile.

*I cannot **believe** the prices they want for the crap in these boutiques! White women just eat this mess up, too! I hope they aren't peddling this same, overpriced garbage on the **Ave**...*

In a bit, she hit the subways, stepped over a derelict (*or two*), hopped on the IND "A" train; and nervously rode back into the temple of her familiar.

This New York was strange to Candace's adult eyes. Back in the Dupont Circle halfway house, all she used to think about was growing up to buy a brownstone in Clinton Hill, Brooklyn; where all the Africentric niggers lived. Those were the niggers who wore the 'Annie Hall' glasses; drove the used 'Beemers' and wore the un-ironed, BLACK BY POPULAR DEMAND tee shirts – through rain snow or gloom of night.

Auntie Aunt was an Africentric nigger. She had a 'stone. Uncle Thurman had a 'stone. 'Stones were neat because when you passed them by it always smelled like somebody was frying chicken. Once you got inside, there was always some random nigger drinking and throwing his two cents in about something Malcolm X was alleged to have testified on one of his albums...

*"If a cat has a kitten in an oven, it ain't no dam **bis**cuit – it's still a gotdam cat! You ain't just **sayin**' it!"*

... Always some ho hollering or laughing in the distance...

*"You got **that** right!"*

... Always some other nondescript nigger yelling "wait jus'a minit" through the bathroom door whenever anybody else had to use it.

*Auntie Aunt liked her scotch with milk and ice, Candace thought; That's fuckin' **nasty**.*

Uncle Thurman swore before Jesus, Mary and Joseph that all he drank was Olde English 800 – but Candace (knee high to a duck, back then) got splashed in her eye more than once behind Uncle Thurman trying to sneak-thief a little Bacardi Dark into his forty ounce.

Candace recalled the severe, almost piercing echoes of gaiety that bounced off the high ceilings of the 'stones. As she walked up Lafayette Avenue and across South Oxford Street in Brooklyn, she remembered her father's car pulling off into the night; her little hand waving 'bye' to all the grownups – and the gaiety – and the 'stones. She remembered the silenced evil that followed them home and shut out the lights in her room. Then, Candace ran from Brooklyn as fast as rapid transit could take her. She was out of breath by the time she reached the Lafayette Ave. subway station; and her hands were bleeding from all that punching against the chiseled bricks of the 'stones.

"I'll be damned." Candace's father was not impressed when she walked in the door. "What the fuck *you* want here? Apparently, my charge wasn't good enough for you when you were younger."

Candace could see that he was still bitter about her dash to D.C. In the early days; but overall her Daddy wasn't so bad, she thought. He was a middle-class nigger with several, notable, fiduciary investments. At the same time, he managed to escape the *house nigger* kind of identity crisis; that makes the *middle-class black man* a criminal in the eyes of the more socio-economically disadvantaged, Africentric, ideology 'police'. He listened to Hip-Hop music; he wore the cheap ten-karat *trunk* gold you could buy *by-the-inch* at the mall. He dusted his 'trunk' chains with the perfunctory, *House* medallion; with the faceted, fake garnet that was stuck somewhere around the head of the Virgin Mary (*If you grew up in New York in the late 70's or early 80's -- you KNOW you know somebody who had one of these!*). Sometimes he would alternate medallions; to one shaped like either marijuana leaves, a city skyline, the African continent or the Island of Jamaica. Pops even had his old, late 70's warm-up suit – for use in case of an emergency trip to the ghetto. He also had a lapel button with Malcolm X's face on it. Whenever he was asked about the button's significance to him, Pops would say, "You just never know when you have to prove you're not a sell-out."

Candace used to have a Malcolm X button, too; though it wasn't the most popular one – the one which showed Malcolm standing by a window with a shotgun – *by any means necessary*. The one *she* had showed El Hajj at Oxford University in England; on the day he addressed the student body (*in regard to American violations of International human rights laws*).

"Hey Dad -- I guess those people at Oxford learned that *intellectual* niggers carry guns, too."

"You got *that* shit right. These days, if you're smart, you *will* carry a gun, Candi. Fuck that shit about the mandatory, one-year jail sentence you get for having a gun in New York State. You can *do* the year."

Candace listened to her father signify;

"Candi. You've got to look at it this way. Wouldn't you rather let the State catch you *with* a gun than some knucklehead criminal catch you *without* one?"

"Gangster whitewalls and Tee-Vee antennas in the back, Daddy," replied Candace; "*School* it, Pimp." They both shared a laugh, but rest assured. Within the week, Candace was sleeping with a serial-shaved, .40 caliber Glock under her bed.

It only took Candace two shakes of a puppy dog's tail (*and her rack in Fred, the hiring manager's face*) to land a job as an apartment rental agent at *Contempo Realty* on East 58th Street; somewhere between Third and Lex.

"*Okay* somebody," yelled Fred from his office door; "We've got an up on line three – answer the damned *phone* already!"

Candace was standing by the desk of one of her coworkers (*Paul*), so she picked up line three from his phone.

"Contempo Realty," she chimed while she used her free hand to swat Paul away. The swat was necessary to stop Paul from giving his monstrous lip-syncing of Candace's telephone salutation. Anyway, she put the call on speaker so that Paul could feel involved.

"Do you still have the apartment that you advertised?" asked the caller.

"In what paper?"

"The *Village Voice.*"

"For how much?" Candace marveled at the way people can call an agency that has a thousand listings; and expect a realtor to site a listing without the slightest bit of specification.

"950," responded the caller, anxiously.

"We have *lots* of apartments in that price range. What's your name?"

"I am Nicolette. I am a model. I am on the cover of *Vogue* this month."

"That's nice." *Who the hell asked her all that,* thought Candace.

"So Nicolette – when do you think you'd like to come in and see some apartments?"

"You have two-bedroom places available, right?"

"Why, *yes.* Yes we do."

Candace hung up the phone, turned directly to Paul and said, "Shut up, Paul! It's not an adventure – it's a *job.*"

"Girlfriend, you can't be serious! This chick thinks she can get two bedrooms for 950 in *Manhattan*? Maybe in Manhattan, *Kansas* – but this ain't Kansas!"

Candace was overjoyed to be able to tell Paul to *shut up* for a second time; "Shut up, Paul. I think Nicolette is coming in this afternoon to see some apartments; and I have no *intention* of showing an apartment less than $1,000-a-month to a *Vogue* magazine cover model." Both agents shared a laugh, then Candace walked back to her desk and sucked on her cup of ice-cold, hot cocoa.

She was gumptious and determined to make something out of this job; no matter *how* many times there was a rub on her shoulder, a pat on her ass or an 'accidental' brush across her nipples from Fred, the boss; or from any of the other men in the office. That being said, she was still, pretty reluctant to use the central, solitary, computer workstation in the office. Her problem was, that in order to have places to show clients, she needed to generate a computer search for eligible apartments in Contempo's database . But -- as sure as the day was long – Candace knew that at least *one* of the men in the office would find a way to move his erection ever-so-slightly across her ass; as soon as she tiptoed to reach the elevated, computer keyboard and monitor.

I ain't even gonna turn around, she thought. *I already* **know** *that the pencil-dick rubbing on my butt cheek right now is my scumbag boss, Fred. Besides – if I cry on the keypad, my makeup will drip on the computer and jam the keys. I guess there's a bright side to this though... half the bitches in this office couldn't get a man's dick hard if they applied paste over it and let it dry under a hi-speed fan!*

Candace laughed aloud for no apparent reason. Other agents and clerks in the office were suffering from their own, telltale symptoms of cerebral menopause; so they didn't pay her outburst much mind.

Nicolette, the model, was supposed to meet up with Candace at the *Contempo* office by 5:30pm. Since Paul had already viewed most of the apartments that Candace's computer search generated, he agreed to tag along and help show them off. If this girl decided to rent one of the units, Candace and Paul would split the difference with the commission (*agents do that all the time; 'cause they have to take the cash where they can get it. I personally, couldn't be a rental agent. Could you?*).

"Yo, *Candace*. By the way... you had keys made to those studio apartments on 89th and York, right?"

"Yeah... "

"Well, why don't you *use* them, sometime. *I'll* spring for the *Mow-Ette*; no *problem*."

Candace laughed at Paul and replied, "Oh, *brother*." Apparently, rental agents did *that* all the time, too.

Nicolette arrived on time; and after a few minutes of departmental explanations and disclaimers, all three of them were off to view the selected apartments. During the ride on the city bus, Candace tried to break the ice of formality between herself and her client; but there wasn't a tissue-ply made *thick* enough to wipe the snot off that big-forehead, no-tits-havin', long-leg, flat-ass, chalk-white bitch.

"The building is about two blocks from here," Paul said as the three of them stepped off the city bus. Five or six minutes later, they were inside a cozy, one-bedroom, duplex apartment; which featured hardwood flooring and a video intercom system.

"Is this all you have?" asked Nicolette, the minute she entered the apartment.

"We've got *plenty* of stuff. Depends on how much you want to *spend*," Paul answered. "Let's take a look around *this* one first, shall we?"

Shall we barf, too? Candace thought.

To be under one thousand per month, this apartment was unarguably attractive. The living room was on the upper level and the single bedroom was downstairs. There were tiled bathrooms on each floor; and the wrought-iron bars that graced the living room's picture window were whimsically crafted to resemble a spider's web.

"So... what do you think, Nicolette? All you need is a sectional sofa and a nice, wall unit," sold Paul; in the tradition of a true, used-car huckster.

"Why is there no electricity here?"

In order to keep from looking completely inept, Candace responded this time; "Well, it's because some landlords do not assume responsibility for Con-Ed in these buildings – other than in common areas like elevators and hallways."

Paul added to what Candace just said, for the close; "Yeah. See, that's why we have these *flashlights*. You just never know which apartments have Con-Ed until you get inside. We are *totally prepared* for these things. *When do you think you can bring us a deposit?*" Candace had to admit that Paul's schlock was in high-art form tonight.

After Nicolette, the model, left the apartment, Candace had an urge to use the bathroom. Normally, she would just wait and use the restroom at a coffee shop, or something; but tonight, she couldn't. The thing is – she'd avoided Mother Nature's calls all day and Mother Nature had become a wee bit perturbed.

"I'll be right out, Paul."

"You *sure* you don't need any help in there? I could hold the flashlight for you... "

"Shut up."

Though there were neither working lights nor windows in the bathrooms of the empty apartment, Candace zoomed into the potty on

the main floor and shut the door. She let out a sigh of **great** satisfaction as she relieved herself for the first time, in that long, wearisome day. She happened to be wearing a full-length, leather trench coat. However, instead of taking it off in the dark, she simply whipped the lower half of the coat up to her lap as she sat on the lavatory. She could hear Paul breathing, so it was obvious that he was standing outside the bathroom door, listening in.

What an idiot. I hope he gags from the smell I'm making in here. Candace wasn't quite finished, but for the sake of having pleasant air to breathe, she flushed the toilet.

"Oh, *shit*," she yelled as the water in the bowl rose to her butt and slowly began to flood the bathroom.

"What's the matter, Candace?" asked Paul.

"This fucking *toilet* is flooding – and I **still have to go!** Oh *shit!*" Candace was *praying* that her previous movements would remain in the privy, in spite of the present overflow.

"Try to hold up that ball in the septic tank; and I'll see if I can open the apartment down the hall with these keys. They're supposed to be *master keys*, y'know."

This is a GOOD one, Candy, she thought to herself; *I have to stand here in the dark with one arm in the septic tank; with pissy water soaking my shoes and riding up my legs – and I still have the urge to poop! Way to get it done!* She was fighting back the flooding of her tears with all full fortitude.

Paul returned quickly and with good news, "*I was* able to open the other apartment after all; and the Con-Ed is *on*. So just come out of there."

For a moment, Candace hesitated. She was well aware of the subtle sexual suggestion that Paul made earlier at the office; but her bladder would not allow her the luxury of pulling her pants up long enough to reach the other, open apartment. So, she took her sopping arm out of the septic tank and wrapped her coat around her body as tightly as she could. Then Candace, with her pants mushed around her ankles, hobbled and wobbled like a Weeble; through the pissy puddle on the parquet floor; out the door and down the hall to the next apartment.

Paul laughed his head off, right in the hallway.

"Wait 'til everybody in the office hears about *this*! You fucked up the bathroom in *one* place – and had to run naked through the building to get to the next place! You'd better hope *this* toilet bowl works, because I didn't test it."

"Shut up, Paul. Just shut the fuck up."

When Candace and Paul returned to the office that evening, their boss was on his way home.

"All I have to say is – either we use the keys to the studio apartments on 87ᵗʰ and York, or I'm telling Fred what happened tonight."

"You wouldn't *dare*, Paul! I'll lose my job!"

Paul was silent and he looked Candace dead in the eye.

No little poo-putt mothafucka is gonna blackmail me like THAT... I'm not going OUT like that! Fuck THAT shit, Candace thought as she stared back at the back-stabber. She made a bee-line for Fred's office and walked in without so much as a knock.

"Fred, before you go, I need to talk to you. It's fairly important."

"Step into my office, cutie. Did I tell you? Your blouse looks *magnificent*."

Maybe if he gets a quick peek at my tits before he leaves, I won't lose my job, Candace considered.

The next day, Paul displayed his anger at losing leverage over Candace by teasing her in public.

"You have an apartment to clean."

"Shit," Candace replied. Next thing you know, everyone in the office was belly-up in laughter.

"Why is everybody laughing? He told you what happened?"

"Yep... he sure *did*... that's so *funny*," said one of the girls who usually was around to make a point -- not to be pleasant to Candace during the course of a day.

"Yes it was," Candace replied, dryly; "And the *funniest* part about it was that I still had to *shit*. Will you all excuse me for a minute? I'm going to take a break." Candace put on her coat, picked up her briefcase and left the raw sewage of the Real Estate world for some *other* over-ambitious knucklehead to flush.

After she'd been back home for about a month or so, Candace realized *why* they called it *Home*. Her father had since moved into her childhood bedroom; but some mornings, she would tiptoe into her old room and watch the day break. After all, it was in this room where she learned that the Sun rises in the East and sets in the West. As long as she kept her life positioned reasonably to the East, the Sun would rise in it, she figured.

This time around however, home just wasn't *Home*. The Indo-Carib Coolies from Guyana and Trinidad had taken *all the way* over. Old Man Abe's soda fountain down the street was now the *Rangpur Deli;* and all the real estate brokerages (*fly-by-fucking-night brokerages, I might add*) had the flags of the proprietor's native country emblazoned on their respective, 'FOR SALE' yard signs. In fact, it had reached the point where if all you could speak was English, it felt like *you* were the outsider.

Candace knew that eventually, she would move back out and try her hand at the world again. When the day finally arrived for her to (*make like a banana and*) split, she knew that telling her dad wasn't going to be easy.

"I'm 'bout to bounce, Daddy," she said as she started down the staircase; "I rented a place in the city... um... and so I'll be back for my stuff... uh... sometime next week, I guess."

As Candace was walking down the steps and stammering, Pops stood at the top of the stairs and stared at her with an *unmistakable* look of **abject, parental disgust** *(that parents the planet-wide, often use in malevolent, malfeasant and mindless attempts to irk, intimidate, and evoke the ire of the world's children)* .

"Come on, Skins. Remember the *old* days, " he said.

Candace recalled her father's intensity – in that he wouldn't say much; he would just smile as she would splash and squeal in the bathtub like a baby. Then, as her wet body would steam in the drafty, household air, Candace would wiggle around on the bed and her father would apply lotion, baby powder and his fingers. He fingered her until she bled.

"Daddy – I know what incest *is*, now. If you touch me again, I'll blow your fucking head off." She walked away from the bottom stair step and moved toward the front door. Pops was still standing at the top of the stairs, though – with that same, stupid look of distorted disgust; speckled – I suppose – with just a dash of demented decadence. Yuck.

"Candi – I thought you *wanted* this house after I die."

Candace stopped; freeze-framed in her tracks. Wouldn't *you*?

See -- in her whole life, she just assumed that no matter *what*, her father would leave her the house. I mean, you know -- like either out of guilt for the sexual abuse or, at least, for the sake of the bloodline. Candace just *knew* that if she'd screwed up her chance to ever own anything in life, she had this old house as a forgiving reprieve. But *no*. Instead, Candace's fuckface of a father had *finally* -- in only **one,** obtuse, obscene, obnoxious and odoriferous oration -- blown her big, blue marble to billions and billions of meaningless bits.

There was an unnatural pause, after ...

... like... a pause of a dying soul, I guess...

"You *win*, Pimpin' -- you win," Candace whimpered as she took her hands off of the front door's handle and threw them up into the gassy air of exasperation. All she could do at that point was walk herself back to the rounded edge of the bottom stair step in the foyer and sit down on it. Pops descended the staircase and approached her where she sat. He had her suck on his dick for a good, *long* while. After he came in her mouth and gagged her (*so that she could could lap up his juice in spite of her locked up jaw*), she went to the *Rangpur Deli* down the street. She thought a grape soda, or a grape Popsicle might wash the distaste out. *Who **you** tellin'? If she **kakalate rite**, she **might** could even git some **asprinnn** wit da change! Shucky ducky, quack, quack! Well – **y'all** know the old sayin' – so go on n' peet afta mee:*

Niggers and Flies,

Niggers and Flies,

The two things I do despise --

The more I see Niggers,

The more I like Flies

As soon as Candace left for the store, "Pimpin'" wiped off his dripping, dangling dick with the tail-end of his dingy, decrepit tee shirt. Then, he took his trifling ass back upstairs in *front-the-TV* and watched the rest of the baseball game-in-progress (*I think the Mets may have been playing Cincinnati... how the* **fuck** *should I know? My imagination is* **hardly** *trying to venture by that fool's bedroom door*).

§

ABOUT THE AUTHOR

This is **LINCOLN PARK'S** second, *sensational* novel.

(Y'all ain't half buy the first one; so we asked her to write another one. LOL!)

Keep up-to-date about what she's working on now at:

www.authorsden.com/lincolnpark

or, visit us/ subscribe to our RSS feed at:

www.4465press.com

~~~